If Only for Tonight

Sherelle Green

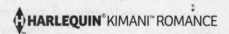

HARLEQUIN® KIMANI™ ROMANCE

To my parents, Carl and Mary, for their unwavering support and unconditional love. The words *thank you* can't justify how grateful I am for all that you both have done for me. You raised me with strong family values and beliefs, always encouraging me to follow my dreams and approach life with confidence and determination. When faced with adversity or an obstacle, you both have overcome. When life throws you a curve ball, you both hit the ball as hard as possible, resulting in a home run. Throughout my life, I've watched you lean on each other for comfort and understanding, always proving that a beautiful relationship like yours—strong…solid…powerful—can withstand *anything*. After thirty years of marriage, you both are the epitome of true love and I'm so honored and blessed to be your daughter.

ISBN-13: 978-0-373-86343-3

IF ONLY FOR TONIGHT

Copyright © 2014 by Sherelle Green

PLEASE RECYCLE
THIS PRODUCT IS RECYCLABLE

Recycling programs for this product may not exist in your area.

HARLEQUIN®

Printed in U.S.A.

www.Harlequin.com

Dear Reader,

Introducing the spiciest owner of Elite Events Incorporated…Cydney Rayne!

I've always admired spontaneous women who aren't afraid to be themselves and seize the moment. I wanted to challenge my fierce heroine by giving her a strong hero who would force her to analyze her views on Mr. Right.

Cyd embodies a sense of mystery and desirability that instantly attracts the devastatingly sexy Shawn Miles. Shawn has always been able to control his feelings and desires, but slowly Cyd begins to uncover the truth behind his facade. Soon, they both realize what may feel so wrong is actually so right!

I'm currently working on Lexus Turner's story, the third installment in the Elite Events series. I love to hear from readers, so please feel free to contact me, and make sure you check out my website for my latest book updates.

Much love,

Sherelle

www.SherelleGreen.com
AuthorSherelleGreen@gmail.com
@SherelleGreen

To my sister, Kelsey, for your support and motivation. When I was crafting the character of Cydney Rayne, I was inspired by your adventurous spirit, mysterious demeanor, intelligence and beauty. You never pass up on an opportunity to enhance yourself culturally and challenge yourself mentally. I greatly admire your drive to live life to its fullest and your ability to always be on the go and not be stagnant in life. As little girls, we shared a bond that could not be broken, and as adults, I'm so elated that our bond has only gotten stronger. You walk with such confidence and embody so many wonderful qualities. I'm so proud to have you as a little sister and I appreciate all the literary inspiration! Without you, Cydney Rayne wouldn't exist. This one's for you, sis!

Prologue

Cydney Rayne enclosed her arms around her body as she inhaled the unique scent of the ocean. On the southeastern coastline of Anguilla, sounds from the sea creatures mingled with those constrained to land as midnight approached.

"So peaceful," Cydney whispered as she closed her eyes and listened to the sound of magnificent waves crashing against the rocky shore. Earlier that day, she'd soaked in the beauty of the bright sunset as it painted the sky a rusty reddish-orange. Now, as she opened her eyes, she admired the splashes of blue and gray that dusted the moon and the brilliant stars shining in the darkness.

Cydney walked over to one of the few light posts on the boardwalk and took off her leather sandals, letting the pinkish sand slide between her toes. Her vacation with her girlfriends from college was finally coming to an end, but she hadn't managed to track down the sexy guy she'd been running into all week. The ladies thought she'd made him up since they hadn't been around to spot him. But she knew she couldn't imagine the naughty conversations she'd had with the stranger or the sensations she felt in her body whenever he was around. She felt more intrigued by this man than any other man from her past. And she didn't even know his name.

She glanced around the deserted beach, wishing she'd brought her iPhone with her to keep track of the time. "Come on, mystery man…where are you?"

Her friends would kill her if they knew she'd sneaked out of the resort at night to track down a man she didn't know. But Cydney was known for being the daredevil of the group. The thrill of danger excited her, and even though her family disliked her adventurous ways sometimes, she couldn't help but be anyone but herself.

Deciding it probably wasn't the best idea to continue to walk around aimlessly in Anguilla, Cydney started to head back to the resort until she noticed she was near the beach house that she'd admired since her arrival. She knew she should keep walking since there weren't any lights surrounding the house, but she slowed down her pace, anyway. All the lights inside the house were off, and according to a local she had queried, the house wasn't occupied. But somehow she sensed someone was in the house, watching her from the front window.

She stood there for a few seconds before a porch light turned on and the front door opened. Out stepped a tall man who appeared to be shirtless. She could barely make out his face in the dim lighting. Her breath caught in her throat. The porch's lighting was just enough for her to tell that he was looking straight at her. She told herself to leave and hurry back to the resort, away from possible danger. But something kept her bare, toenail-polished feet planted in the sand as her blue summer dress danced in the night wind.

He stepped off the porch and began taking slow, purposeful steps toward her. A closer look at the man made her heart beat even faster. As he drew nearer, she told herself to be prepared for anything that the night had in store. After all, that was what she'd ventured to the beach for. She'd wanted to find her sexy mystery man, and there he was…in the flesh.

"So we meet again," he said in an alluring voice as he approached her.

"I guess so. You told me you'd be on the beach, but I didn't expect to find you in a deserted beach house."

The amused look on his face was undeniable.

"You didn't think I'd come, did you?"

"Not really," he said with a smile. "Beautiful women don't often go out into the night to meet a stranger they haven't even been formally introduced to."

What he said was definitely true considering she'd questioned her own motives several times while walking along the beach.

"Well, I guess I'm not most beautiful women then, am I?"

He walked closer to her and she confirmed her observation. He wasn't wearing a shirt, allowing her a nice view of his delectable six-pack.

"I guess not," he answered, studying her, as well. "My name is Brandon. It's nice to meet you," he continued. He offered a handshake as he removed one hand from the pockets of his khaki shorts.

Cydney wondered if she should give him her real name but decided against it. "Nice to meet you, Brandon. My name is Jessica."

She returned his handshake and felt an electric spark the minute their hands touched. She was totally caught off guard by the feeling and immediately dropped his hand. His eyes glinted with amusement.

"Very nice to meet you, too, Jessica. And might I add, I've enjoyed the conversations we've had this past week. Honestly, I can't say I've ever been this captivated by a woman before."

Cydney felt the same way but couldn't explain why she'd felt compelled to exchange naughty dialogues with the stranger. In fact, she'd been the one to start the conversations. She'd first seen him at a food market where he'd been buying coconut cake, a local dessert extremely well-known on the island. She'd waited until he was leaving, and being the daring person she was, she'd told him she'd love to lick the dessert off his body and then walked away, leaving him with a stunned look on his face.

He'd returned the favor the next day by walking into a local clothing store while she was shopping and saying he'd love for her to purchase the swimsuit she had in her hands just so that he could strip it off her later. He'd taken it one step further and explained everything he would do to her naked body.

Their back-and-forth naughty banter had continued every time they'd seen each other until finally he'd told her to meet him on the beach her last night in Anguilla. That night had finally come, and she didn't know if she was spontaneous or foolish for meeting with a man who had *just* learned her *name,* but probably remembered all the sexual positions she whispered in his ear for the past week.

"Brandon, I want you to know that I've never done

anything like this before," Cydney blurted out, although she wasn't sure why she cared since she didn't plan to ever see him again.

He grazed her cheek with the back of his hand. "I know. Believe it or not, I know what type of woman you are."

The gesture was sweet, but Cydney didn't believe him. What woman would believe a man in her position? She knew what he wanted, and it was fine with her because she wanted the same thing. She'd never had a one-night stand, but she didn't think she could stop herself now, even if she tried. The man was definitely in shape and had the build of a basketball player. His skin was the color of cinnamon and she'd never seen eyes like his. They weren't hazel or blue but more so a combination of the two. Sea-blue, she thought as she peered a little closer. He was hot....

"So what do you say, Jessica?" he said, breaking into her thoughts. "Will you come inside the beach house and spend the night with me?"

Cydney looked him up and down, her eyes lingering on his six-pack. *How can I say no to a man this fine?* She didn't live with regrets and after one more glance over his body, she knew she'd regret not taking him up on his offer.

"I accept," Cydney said, relishing in the desire reflected in his eyes. "But only on one condition."

"What's that?" Brandon said, his voice even sexier than before.

Cydney tilted her head to the side as she observed Brandon a little more closely. She was one day shy of twenty-seven and definitely not a stranger to the bedroom. But there were still certain things that she'd always wanted to try yet never entertained with other men. If only for tonight, she wanted to live out one of her fantasies. She glanced at the beach, and then back at Brandon.

"I want to have sex in the ocean," Cydney finally replied.

Brandon smiled at her and nodded his head in agreement. "That seems simple enough."

"But not just that," Cydney continued. "I want us to continue our naughty conversations by talking dirty while we explain every single thing we want to do to each other…while having sex in the ocean. No inhibitions…."

Cydney watched the fire build up in his eyes right before he stepped closer to her. His hands gently grazed her face again, only this time they didn't stop there. He took one finger and dragged it in between her cleavage before dropping his head to the side of her neck. There, he placed soft kisses along her neckline, paying close attention to the parts right above her breasts. Cydney dropped her head back and enjoyed the way his lips felt on her skin. She couldn't help the moans that escaped her mouth with every seductive kiss he placed on her upper body.

When he neared her mouth, she stopped him before their lips could touch. Outlining his jawline with her finger, she used her free hand to gently push him away from her. She took that moment to provocatively lift her dress over her head, revealing her spicy two-piece bathing suit.

Her eyes were pinned to his lips as he licked them in anticipation and slowly unzipped his pants before pushing them completely off. Cydney gasped at the sight that was before her. Brandon hadn't worn anything underneath, displaying his enlarged sex. Her mouth watered as she took in the complete sight of his sexy nakedness. His arms and abs were so muscular that it made her want to lick every crevice of his body like it was a chocolate-ice-cream sundae.

He walked toward her, one mission clearly evident in his mind. Instead of getting nervous, Cydney flirtatiously smiled and met him halfway.

"I see you brought the swimsuit you were looking at in the store," Brandon said as he played with the string on the side of her bikini.

"I always keep my promises," Cydney replied, her voice catching as his eyes grew even deeper with desire.

"Come with me," he told her seductively while grabbing her hand and leading her to the ocean. Her inner voice warned her that a man this sexy could be dangerous for a woman's psyche. Men this fine were hard to forget and even harder to duplicate. But that inner voice was no longer present the minute their bodies hit the water. The only thought on Cydney's mind was making sure she remembered every moment she spent with her sexy island lover.

Chapter 1

Eight months later...

"Cydney Rayne."

She glanced up at the man who had whispered her name and prayed her eyes were deceiving her. They'd been formally introduced an hour before her sister Imani's wedding, and her body temperature still hadn't returned to normal. It had taken all her strength to stand up as maid of honor and not steal glances at the sexy man whose eyes had been glued to her the entire ceremony.

Imani and Daman Barker's backyard wedding reception was in full swing, and she didn't dare regard the man while being surrounded by her family and friends.

"Please follow me," she said quickly before leaving the reception and retreating to a nearby walk-in closet inside her grandfather's large house. As soon as she shut the closet door, she wondered why she hadn't found a less confined hiding spot.

As they stood there observing one another, she wondered who would be the first to speak. *Goodness, the man looked devastatingly sexy.* He looked even better than she remembered. His black suit looked tailor-made and now the foremost thought in her mind was how good he'd look out of it.

He licked his lips as his eyes practically burned a hole through her lavender maid-of-honor dress. He was obviously having the same thoughts she was. She wanted to kiss him badly, and seeing the fire in his eyes, she knew that he wanted to kiss her, too. But Cydney refused to start something with a man like him—the kind of man who oozed sex appeal and looked like he just walked off the cover of *GQ* magazine. She could lose her damn mind with a man like him, and losing her sanity over a man, no matter how good he looked, was *not* an option.

A month ago, when she'd gone to help her new brother-in-law move out of his Detroit condo, she had seen a picture of Daman with a man she couldn't quite make out. She could only see his profile in the picture, but she instantly knew that she had met the man previously. Refusing to believe her eyes, she put the photo out of her mind, hoping it was just a weird coincidence that he resembled *that* man she'd tried to forget about. Now, staring back into a pair of amused sea-blue eyes, she reminded herself that she never did believe in coincidences.

"So, Cydney Rayne, would you like me to call you Jessica, Cydney or do you prefer Cyd, the name everyone else has been calling you all day?"

She wished she could wipe that smirk off his handsome face. She wasn't the only one who'd made up a fake name. "Well, that depends. Do you want me to call you Shawn Miles or would you rather I call you Brandon?"

His eyes squinted together. "Although I loved the way you screamed my name that night in the ocean, I'd wished you were screaming Shawn rather than Brandon. Now that you know my real name, maybe we can make that happen."

Throwing her head back in an exaggerated laugh, she refused to let his arrogance get to her. "I'm sure your ears were playing tricks on you, but if that's the name your mother gave you, then Shawn it is. You can call me Cyd or Cydney, but if you think for one minute that we'll be sleeping together, think again."

He was still smiling and checking her out. She tried to keep a calm demeanor, but she was anything but relaxed. She couldn't even remember how Shawn knew Daman since she hadn't really listened to the introductions past learning his real name. The moment she'd seen his face before the wedding, she'd wanted to crawl into a deep, dark hole. However, Shawn had looked more amused than surprised. She'd barely returned his handshake when the enormity of the situation had hit her full force. Most people never saw their one-night stands again. Unfortunately for Cyd, her one-night stand came strolling through her grandfather's backyard for her sister's wedding. *Seriously?*

"How *do* you know Daman, anyway?"

He looked at her from head to toe one more time before responding. "I met Daman through Malik Madden, a mutual friend."

Cyd wondered if Shawn had known her true identity when they'd first met on the island.

"No, I didn't know we shared a mutual friend. Imani

and Daman hadn't started working on the gala they planned yet," Shawn said, interjecting her thoughts.

Cyd squinted her eyes together, soaking in his accurate assessment. "I didn't even ask you anything," she snapped. Even if he didn't know her then, she was sure he'd known about her before he got to the wedding because he hadn't appeared surprised when he saw her.

"You're right. I knew who you were before I got here today. After meeting with Daman and Malik one day, I used Google to search Imani when I heard she was marrying Daman. That's when I spotted a picture of you and your business partners."

Cyd rolled her eyes and shook her head when he read her thoughts once more. Clearly Shawn had done his research. Cyd, along with her sister Imani Rayne-Barker, cousin Lexus Turner and friend Mya Winters were proud founders of Elite Events, Incorporated in Chicago. The women were well-known for planning elaborate events that left lasting impressions with all who had the pleasure of attending.

"How do you know that's what I'm thinking? I could have been thinking anything." Cyd didn't like when people assumed they knew what was on her mind because usually they were wrong in their assumptions. But Shawn had correctly assessed her thoughts, and that didn't sit well with her.

Shawn pushed aside a coat that was partially blocking his view of Cyd. "That's true, but you weren't just thinking anything. And trust me, Cyd, I wanted to track you down the minute I found the information."

He was really starting to irritate her. He spoke to her as if they'd known each other forever instead of just being sex partners for one night. "Listen, you don't know me, Shawn Miles, or whatever your name is. So do us both a favor and stop acting like you do."

He leaned in closer, and she inhaled his enticing masculine scent. Being around him was a threat to her sanity, and her body was a ball of nerves. Her heart beat even faster as her eyes followed his hand that reached for her face. She couldn't help but lean into him a little more.

"I know you better than you think, Cydney Rayne or Jessica or *whatever your name is.* And I also noticed your hair. It's different than I remember. This color makes you look even sexier than you did the week we met."

His voice was so seductive that she squeezed her thighs tighter to try to ease the ache that was starting to develop. When she'd met Shawn, her hair had been light brown and styled in natural waves since she'd wanted a look suited for the island. Now her hair was jet-black and cut in soft layers that flowed around her shoulders. The dark color looked dramatic on her light butter-toffee complexion, and she'd definitely gotten a lot more attention since she'd dyed it.

Cyd slowly backed up into a corner of the closet, attempting to put some distance between them. Refusing to give her space, Shawn followed her into the corner and brushed a few fallen strands of hair out of her face with the back of his hand. The heat in the closet rose twenty degrees, and for the second time, she wished she hadn't chosen a closet as their hiding place. He leaned in, indicating that he was going to kiss her. She could feel it and even worse, she wanted it.

"What are you doing?" she asked, a little more breathless than she would have liked.

"If you have to ask, then I must be doing something wrong."

No, he was definitely doing everything right. But she was trying to stall the passionate explosion that she knew would come from his kiss. His six-foot-three-inch frame towered over her five-foot-nine-inch body. He'd successfully blocked her from any route of escape.

As his face grew closer to hers, she didn't have the willpower to stop him.

"I've been waiting to do this for eight months," he said as he dipped his head to hers. The moment their lips touched, she felt the burst of passion she'd been waiting for. Her tongue mated with his as she reacquainted herself with his savory taste. His hands went around her waist and straight to her backside as she wrapped her arms around his neck. When Shawn began to grind against her core, she lost all sense of reality. The fact that he had such a strong sexual hold on her was extremely unsettling.

When her back hit the closet wall, she lifted her right leg and was rewarded by his strong, masculine hand grasping her thigh to keep her in place. His hands were like fire as her body melted to his every caress. She was pretty sure she could come on the spot without him even trying. *That* was how badly she wanted Shawn.

"Cydney," Shawn said breathlessly in between kisses, "if we don't stop soon, I'm taking you right here, right now, no ifs, ands or buts about it. Like I said, I've waited eight months to do this, and after kissing you, all I want to do is fill myself with the sweet taste of you."

He pulled her even closer so she could feel his manhood press against the spot he wanted to bury himself inside. Cyd was so aroused, she could barely think.

She knew what she wanted, but she also knew that she shouldn't succumb to it. *Then again, when do I ever do what I should?* Being the bold person she was made the answer easy.

"Well, Shawn, if you think you can still handle me, by all means…*prove it.*"

She was thinking with the lower part of her body but this time she didn't care. She inched onto the tiptoes of her left foot and Shawn quickly lifted her so that both of her thighs were in his palms. A rush of anticipation shot through her body as she leaned against the wall while he pushed her dress high on her waist and tightened his grip even more.

Cyd assumed he'd just get down to business, but instead, Shawn leaned into her, licking from the base of her collarbone to the middle of her neck, leaving a trail of soft, wet kisses along the way. He methodically began grinding against her core while his hands gripped her butt, bringing her closer to the fit of him.

She wrapped her legs tighter around Shawn's waist as she gripped one of the closet poles to maintain her balance. When his lips found hers again, she was hungry and waiting. She could taste the remnants of wine on his lips, heightening her aroused state. She tried to think of any reason why she should stop Shawn from moving any further, but her mind was void of excuses. This man, her island lover with the cinnamon-colored skin and abs hard enough to bounce quarters off, was what all wet fantasies were made of. She couldn't deny herself the opportunity to make love to a man guaranteed to take her on a journey to ecstasy.

Cyd tore off his jacket and Shawn wasted no time tearing off his dress shirt and throwing it aside, as well.

His sexy arms flexed with each movement of their bodies and he never once let her feet touch the floor in his hastiness to remove his clothes.

Shawn reached in his back pocket and ripped open a condom packet. Cyd unzipped his pants and quickly put the condom in place, briefly massaging his member as she slid the condom over his shaft.

"I see you're prepared," Cyd murmured between kisses.

"Don't forget that I knew you would be here and I was hoping I'd get a chance to talk to you. I figured with you, I'd better be prepared for anything."

She wasn't sure if she liked the fact that he was prepared or offended that he thought there was a possibility they would have sex again.

"I guess if I think about the last time we were together, it makes sense that you were prepared."

Shawn stopped kissing her neck and gazed into her chestnut-brown eyes. She felt like she was under a microscope and her uneasiness increased when she couldn't make out his thoughts.

"I was hoping I'd be lucky enough to have another moment with you," Shawn said while rubbing his hands along her thighs. "I never forgot about the last time we were together, and I hung on to that hope that maybe you felt the same way about me and wanted to share another intimate moment. I didn't assume, but I damn sure hoped you did."

She melted at his reply. *Lord, help me.* The man had a way with words and she was being baited by his charm. Cyd always prided herself on knowing the difference between a man running game on her and a man genuinely expressing his feelings. Shawn was being genuine and the sincerity in his eyes was undeniable. But she couldn't get too wrapped up in the emotions she felt. This was only about sex. Instead of responding to his words, she adjusted herself and slowly guided his shaft into her core until he reached her hilt.

Shawn exhaled deeply and took over from there, gliding in and out of her wet center with ease. This was the moment she'd missed since their last encounter. This was the feeling she'd dreamed about, the sensations she knew only he could provide.

They'd been exchanging words since they'd stepped into the closet, but at this moment all words ceased. Shawn's eyes stared into Cyd's with an intensity she felt throughout her entire body. There was nothing sexier than a shirtless man sexing the hell out of a woman with his body and his eyes. All the coats and shirts hanging in the closet rocked back and forth to the movement of their hips.

Shawn never lost eye contact with her. There was never a man who wanted her this badly. The fact that he was so honest about his desire excited and scared her all at the same time. *Damn, what is it about this man?* Cyd had had good sex, but none of her past partners remotely compared to Shawn. Not even close.

Her orgasm was threatening to break free and Shawn increased his pace. She gripped his shoulders to maintain her balance as her body lifted more toward the ceiling with each powerful thrust into her core.

"Shawn," Cyd whispered. "We've been in this closet for a while and I know my family is wondering where I am. This time has to be a quickie."

She'd quickly realized her mistake in implying that they would have sex again in the future. The sly smile on his face proved that he'd caught her mishap and wouldn't let her forget about the implication.

"Who am I to disappoint," Shawn said, his eyes briefly lowering to admire the healthy amount of cleavage bursting through the top of her dress. There they were again, those slick words and that sexy look that had her insides twirling in a massive heap of desire.

"I want you to look me in the eyes as you come," Shawn whispered in her ear. Although she didn't want to, she obeyed his request and stared deeply into his sea-blue eyes. That was her undoing. The look in his eyes told her that even though this was a quickie, he was far from finished with her. In the time she'd shared with Shawn eight months ago, she'd realized he was a man who said what he meant and meant what he said. There was no doubt in her mind that they would have sex again, and she wouldn't even bother convincing herself otherwise.

"Cydney, it's time," Shawn said in a husky voice a little louder than before. Her faint moans were growing louder and on instinct, Shawn pinned her up on the wall even harder using only his thighs to hold her up while one hand gently covered her mouth. The movement brought him even deeper inside her and soon she mirrored his technique and covered his mouth to conceal his loud groans. Only using one hand for balance, Cyd bounced up and down as Shawn came completely out of her center only to bring her back down on him. He thrust harder twice more until they both released the passion they'd been holding inside. Cyd wanted to close her eyes as she became overcome with emotions she hadn't felt in months, but she kept her eyes open. She had no choice. Shawn was still staring at her, still embedded deep in her core, warning her that this was only the beginning. He had plans for her, or at least her body. And with a man like him, she knew she had to stand her ground or give in to temptation.

Chapter 2

Seductive moans swarmed around in Shawn's memory as he recalled every delicate feature of Cydney's curves. He should have been paying attention to the current topic of discussion at his weekly meeting, but he couldn't get his mind off her. For months, he'd dreamed about the unbelievable sex he'd had with his exotic lover, and this past weekend he'd sampled her sweetness again.

When he'd learned her identity a month ago, he'd wanted to contact her right away but he didn't think she'd respond well, since like him, she assumed they'd never see each other again.

I wonder what brought her to Anguilla eight months ago. He'd planned to ask her after they were formally introduced. But when he saw her, the only thing on his mind was getting her out of her dress. She'd looked even sexier than he remembered and he wasn't done with her yet. Far from it.

An undercover FBI assignment had led him to Chicago and he was definitely going to make the most of his time here after he solved the case. He'd need a good distraction after the upcoming months he faced, anyway. This case was one of the biggest of his career and for personal reasons, it was one of the most important.

"That's all for now, folks," said Chicago senior supervisory special agent Larry Wolfe as the meeting came to a close. "Shawn, can you follow me to my office?"

"Yes sir," Shawn said, putting his thoughts of Cydney on hold. When they arrived at the office, Shawn took a seat close to a window.

"Shawn, I wanted to talk to you about the assignment in a little more detail," Agent Wolfe said as he sat in a large desk chair opposite Shawn. "I'm sure I don't have to remind you how important this case is. The DEA and Chicago P.D. will be working closely with us. I know you've researched all the current employees for the Peter Vallant Company, but as acting chief information security officer, you need to be debriefed on all the new employees and volunteers for the company."

Agent Wolfe opened the top shelf of his file cabinet and pulled out a manila file folder. "I need you to go over everything in this file. As you know, Mr. Peter Vallant is the owner of the Peter Vallant Company, one of the top real estate firms in the nation. Mr. Vallant is throwing a series of customer appreciation events in Illinois and Indiana to thank all of the company's supporters and contributors who participated in their Rebuild Your Community program initiative. You'll be attending every event and Mr. Vallant is aware that you are undercover. He has agreed to assist you with any additional information you need while attending the events. I trust that your team is prepared."

"Yes, sir. My top four security guards are aware of

the situation and will provide extra sets of eyes during the tour for any suspicious activity. The rest of my security team will stay in Chicago and were told to be alert as they are with every security matter we handle." In addition to working with the FBI, Shawn had spent the past year building his own high-level security firm. He hadn't decided on a city to headquarter his company, but he had hired a top-notch security team of former members of the FBI, CIA, P.D. and U.S. military.

"Good. They leave on the appreciation tour later this week."

"I'll be ready," Shawn said as he stood from his seat.

"Oh, and, Shawn," Agent Wolfe called.

"Yes," Shawn said as he turned his head over his shoulder.

"Can you handle this?"

Shawn knew why he was asking and appreciated the concern. But there was no way he was giving up the opportunity to work on this case. He stood to lose too much and he knew that solving the case would bring him some closure. "Is there anything I can't handle?" he said sarcastically, demeaning the seriousness of the situation.

"Just making sure," Agent Wolfe said with a slight laugh.

Shawn then walked out of the office and into the busy hallway buzzing with agents and other personnel ready to start their Monday. Using his thumb to flip through the pages in the file, Shawn familiarized himself with a few new faces he hadn't originally researched as he shuffled around people walking past him.

When he was halfway through glancing at the

pages in the file, Shawn stopped short. "What are the odds," he said surprisingly as he studied the beautiful brown eyes of the woman who'd been sneaking into his thoughts way too frequently.

"Cydney Rayne, Elite Events, Incorporated. Lead planner for the appreciation series of events," Shawn said aloud as he read the headline on the page. "Damn." Yes, he was anxious to see her and continue what they'd started in the closet, but he didn't mix business with pleasure. When it came to his work, nothing and no one stood in his way, and he couldn't afford to compromise this case.

Shawn had a reputation as being one of the best undercover special agents in the bureau. A lot of agents were surprised to learn he ultimately wanted to leave the FBI and start his own company. But those who knew his story weren't surprised by his decision at all. For the past few years he'd tried to avoid coming back to Chicago, the second city he was assigned to when he joined the FBI. But a few months ago, he'd known he had to return and finish what he'd started. It was a miracle he even got on this case in the first place. Agent Wolfe was more than his supervisor. He was more like family. Shawn hadn't had the pleasure of knowing his biological parents and although he had great guardians, Agent Wolfe had been key in his development from boy to man. Agent Wolfe knew what Shawn stood to lose if he didn't solve the case, and since he cared about him, Agent Wolfe had appointed Shawn as the undercover agent despite the personal conflict. But Shawn wasn't too sure how Agent Wolfe would react if he knew about his relationship with Cydney.

"Miss Rayne, Miss Rayne. It seems I have a bigger

issue than I thought," Shawn said as he continued to stare intently at her picture. Since their relationship had been purely physical, he hadn't told her what he did for a living. He would have given her a fake job, anyway, but that would have further complicated the situation, so he was glad that he had kept his mouth shut. Cydney wouldn't like the fact that she would be working so closely with him, so she'd probably maintain her distance. At least that was what Shawn was hoping would be the case. He had a feeling that Cydney could be unpredictable at times and that could definitely pose a problem.

He looked from her eyes to her lips as he studied her picture one last time. For his sake, he hoped she would decide to keep her distance because if she didn't, he wasn't sure if he'd be able to resist her.

"Stay focused," he said to himself as he tried to reinforce his thoughts before leaving her page to finish scanning the rest of the documents in the file.

Cyd chanted Beyoncé's recent hit as she poured herself a cup of coffee and waited for her partners to arrive to the conference room. The song had been playing in her head all weekend and she was feeling good. Even better than good—she was feeling great. She wanted to ignore the fact that Shawn was the cause of her happiness, but she couldn't. The man had sexed her in a much needed way and she'd been on a high ever since.

After adding the perfect amount of cream and sugar to her coffee, she took a sip and savored the bitter yet sweet taste. She walked to a nearby window to enjoy the brilliant colors of the fall leaves, taking two more sips of the warm deliciousness. Each taste was better than the last.

"Hmm," she said aloud, not noticing that her partners had walked into the conference room. "Amazing."

"Okay," her sister Imani said, disrupting her enjoyable moment. "Who are you and what have you done with the real Cydney Rayne?"

"Very funny," Cyd replied. "I haven't been that bad."

Imani looked at Mya and Lex before turning her head back to Cyd. "You're joking, right? Do you even remember how you've been acting lately?"

"Well, let us remind you," Lex chimed in. "You've been tense over the past few months even though you've tried to hide it behind your usual sarcasm. To make matters worse, you missed the bridesmaids' group dance and the maid-of-honor toast on Imani's wedding day."

Whoops! Cyd had definitely forgotten about those last couple details. "Hey, I gave my maid-of-honor toast."

"Yeah, about thirty minutes late!" Mya replied. "And you disappeared for almost an hour. We couldn't find you anywhere."

"So true," Imani added. "Even though I refused to get upset on the most important day of my life, I honestly can't believe you pulled a stunt like that on my wedding day."

Cyd dropped her head backward and stared at the ceiling. She was slightly irritated that she was receiving the third degree, although part of her knew she deserved it. As she twisted her head to crack her neck, she immediately thought about Shawn placing soft kisses along her collarbone. She could still visualize every single moment of their sexual escapade in the closet.

"And you have the nerve to be smiling right now," Imani said, interrupting her thoughts. "Oh, man, you are so lucky that I leave for my honeymoon in a few days because I could strangle you! But I refuse to get arrested and miss my vacation with my new husband!"

"Sorry," Cyd said as she sat down at the conference table and thought about how her sister must feel. "If it's any consolation, I have a very good explanation."

All three women joined her at the table as they waited intently for her to finish.

"We're listening," Imani said impatiently when Cyd didn't jump right in with excuses. Cyd had planned on telling them about Shawn, but she was hoping they would be a little less tense if she waited until Monday. Times like this made working with her sister, cousin and friend really complicated. They were a large part of one another's lives and were also founders of a very successful business. Although she loved them dearly, sometimes she wished she could have a day or two to relax and take a step back from the family and business chaos. Luckily, a series of upcoming events would help her do just that.

Taking a deep breath, Cyd put on her big-girl pants and prepared to explain what happened.

"Do you guys remember meeting Shawn at the wedding?"

"Daman's friend?" Imani asked.

"Yes," Cyd replied as she watched each of her partner's eyes open wide with interest. "Well, something happened between us during the wedding."

"And what exactly might that be?" Mya inquired.

Cyd scrunched her nose as she thought about the right way to tell them. Slightly closing her eyes, she chose to be blunt about it. "We sneaked off to the grand walk-in closet in the foyer…and had sex." There, she'd said it.

As she fully opened her eyes, she laughed when she noticed all three women had their mouths hanging open.

Imani was the first to speak. "You mean to tell me that while I was wondering why on earth my sister and maid of honor had missed our group dance and the time for her speech, you were getting freaky in a closet?"

"Um…yes," Cyd said a little unknowingly, since she couldn't tell if her sister's high-pitched squeal and the fact that she was now standing was a good or bad thing.

Imani's face went from surprise to excitement in a matter of seconds. "Well, judging how fine Shawn is, I'd say you did well, little sis."

Cyd threw her head back and laughed. She should have known her sister would react that way.

"I shouldn't even have to ask based off that look you had a few minutes ago, but was the sex good?"

Cyd gripped her Starbucks mug a little tighter and took another sip of her coffee. "It was way better than good. Y'all saw how the man looked that day. I could barely control myself when we were introduced." No need to disclose the fact that it had actually been their second time meeting each other. She'd keep that bit of information to herself.

"He had to be good," Lex interjected. "I never remember you actually giving a man credit for being better than good in the bedroom."

"Or admit to not being able to control yourself," Imani added. "So I'm guessing he had a lot of qualities off your list?"

Instead of answering Imani's question, Cyd's mind

drifted back to the night she was with Shawn in Anguilla. She had spent a week with Imani, Lex and Mya in Barbados before meeting her college girlfriends in Anguilla. Lex and Mya had been on a quest to find sexy islanders in Barbados and had succeeded. But nothing could have prepared her for the likes of Shawn Miles when she landed in Anguilla. As shallow as it sounded, Cyd always knew the men she entertained weren't up to her standard. The men who she believed were a great match were often too nervous to approach her, further proving her point that he wasn't "Mr. Right" in the first place. So she settled for a bunch of "Mr. Right Nows," waiting for a man who would sweep her off her feet.

Imani cleared her throat, zapping Cyd back to reality. "No," Cyd slightly lied. "He doesn't have a lot of qualities on my love list, but he does have almost every quality off my lust list."

"Maybe you should create a 'you're full of it' list," Mya said with a laugh, her comment receiving snickers from Imani and Lex, as well. Cyd knew they thought her lists were stupid, but she didn't care. In her mind, her lists were a necessity.

"Don't we have business to discuss?" Cyd said, directing her question to Imani since it was her turn to lead the meeting. Imani gave her a look insinuating that she wanted to say something else, but luckily she dropped it.

"Okay, since Cyd will have her hands tied with the series of appreciation events for the Peter Vallant Company, we will need to make sure we plan efficiently and not overbook ourselves."

"Agreed," Mya said. "Let's make sure that we remind our assistants to constantly check our calendars."

"How much traveling is required?" Lex asked Cyd.

"Since the events are all in Illinois or Indiana, I will be living in and out of a hotel for the next month or so, but I don't mind. I'll find out more when I meet with Mr. Vallant in a couple days." Cyd loved to travel, and although small towns in the Midwest weren't exactly her idea of a good time, she'd enjoy herself nonetheless.

"Great. How about we go around the table and give an update on what we're working on," Imani suggested. "I'll go first."

Chapter 3

"Oh, my goodness, please let the weather stay this warm," Cyd said to the sky as she walked down the busy streets of Chicago's West Loop wearing her favorite designer sunglasses. The sunny October weather was unlike any she'd ever experienced in Chicago and she was enjoying every minute of it.

This afternoon she was meeting with Mr. Vallant to get the final details on the appreciation event tour for the Rebuild Your Community initiative. Elite Events, Incorporated was extremely honored to plan the events and Cyd was very proud of the agenda she'd created for each occasion on the tour.

She dodged through walkers, making sure she didn't roll over anyone's feet with her suitcase. "On your left," yelled a biker who was forced to use the sidewalks due to heavy traffic and street construction. Since the weather was so nice, Chicago construction was at its highest after the city decided to restructure several major streets in Chicago's West and South Loops. Cyd was glad she'd worn her most comfortable black high-waist skirt and heels. She'd completed her outfit with a teal blouse and complementing accessories.

Reaching her destination, she promptly signed the visitor logbook and waited in the tastefully decorated lobby for Mr. Vallant's assistant.

"Ms. Rayne?" said a woman with a questioning, raspy voice.

"Yes, I'm Cydney Rayne," Cyd replied as she shook hands with the woman. The woman didn't say anything at first, but observed her so intently, Cyd felt as if she were under a microscope.

"My name is Verona Neely and I'm Mr. Vallant's assistant," she said, her awkward demeanor growing perky in a matter of seconds. "Mr. Vallant invited a few other individuals to the meeting and he apologizes for not telling you about this change sooner. Please follow me to the conference room."

"Thank you, Ms. Neely."

When they arrived at the conference room with tall, floor-to-ceiling windows overlooking Lake Michigan, seven people were already seated at a large table. Cyd placed her belongings on a counter off to the side of the room.

"Ms. Rayne," said Mr. Vallant as he stood to shake her hand. "Allow me to introduce you to a few members of my executive team. We have Kim Lathers, chief marketing officer. Jim Pearson, senior vice president of business development. Jacob Early, chief financial officer. Brittany Higgins, senior vice president of client services. Tom Mendez, senior vice president of communications and Paul Jensen, general counsel. Everyone, this is Cydney Rayne from Elite Events, Incorporated."

Cyd made her way around the table as she shook

hands with each member before taking a seat in one of two vacancies. "Nice to meet you all."

"Throughout the next month members of the executive team will be present at a few of the appreciation events. I felt it best that we all attend this meeting to ensure that everyone understands the schedule. Team, I trust that you will make Ms. Rayne feel welcome during the tour."

Everyone nodded their heads in agreement and exchanged a few warm words. Adjusting herself in her seat, she tried to place the reason behind her suddenly quickened heartbeat. Her heart only beat this fast when she was nervous, but she usually never got nervous on the job. She momentarily stopped observing her behavior when she heard the conference door open. *No way.... No freaking way.* Now it all made sense. There was one new development in her life that seemed to be wreaking havoc on her nerves since the day she'd laid eyes on him.

"Ms. Rayne. This is the newest member of our team, Shawn Miles, chief information security officer," Mr. Vallant said, rising once again from his chair to make the introduction. "Shawn, please meet Cydney Rayne from Elite Events, Incorporated."

"Nice to meet you, Ms. Rayne," Shawn said with ease, once again giving himself away and proving that he wasn't surprised to see her at all. *Of course Shawn works for the Peter Vallant Company,* she thought sarcastically. What was it with this man! How did he manage to pop up in her life not once, not twice, but three times!

"Nice to meet you, too, Mr. Miles," Cyd replied, accepting his handshake and ignoring the electric surge that shot through her arm. He looked great in his navy blue suit, but she refused to give him a compliment. He never told her what he did for a living, but he'd admitted to researching her online. She guessed it was partially her fault for not researching him online, too. She'd much preferred to keep him a mystery, but had she just searched his name on the internet, she could have saved herself some embarrassment.

She was so sick and tired of Shawn getting the upper hand. Even if he was new to the company, he'd probably been told that she would be the lead planner for the appreciation tour. Cyd nervously glanced around the table before her eyes settled back on Shawn. She wished he'd wipe that smirk off his face. Better yet, she wished she could punch it off him. But Cyd had way more class than that.

"Let's all take a seat," Mr. Vallant said as he returned to his chair. As Cyd sat back down, she twisted in her seat so that her back was slightly to Shawn, directing her full attention to Mr. Vallant at the head of the table.

"I'll begin our discussion with the rotation schedule for the events. As lead event planner, Ms. Rayne will be attending every event. Here is the schedule for the rest of the events," Mr. Vallant said as he directed his attention at the material that had been placed in front of each attendee's seat.

Cyd didn't hear Mr. Vallant announce that as CISO, Shawn would also be present at every event, though a quick scan of the document made that fact evident, anyway. The hairs on the back of her neck stood on high awareness as Shawn leaned forward to pick up something he'd dropped on the floor. She sighed a little deeper than necessary as she gripped the mahogany table while uncrossing her legs just to cross them back again.

There it was again. The butterflies she couldn't stop from swarming in the pit of her stomach. Yet she managed to answer every question that was directed at her during the course of the meeting. Though she wasn't sure how she answered anything at all, given all her attention was secretly fixed on the man to the right.

She glanced at the clock on the wall and prayed that the already forty-minutes-long meeting would conclude in the next twenty minutes. She looked through a folder that Mr. Vallant had handed her a few minutes prior to see the list of hotels she would be staying at during the appreciation tour. Over the next month, there would be four stops. Cyd lived in downtown Chicago, but tonight she would be staying at the JW Marriott, host hotel for the Peter Vallant reception for the employees to thank them for all their hard work. On Friday, they left for their first stop, Springfield, Illinois.

At the sound of Shawn's voice, Cyd turned her head to listen to what he was saying, as did everyone at the table. She wanted to comprehend his words, but she couldn't. His lips looked too sexy today. He stuck his tongue in and out between sentences to moisten his lips, glancing at her after every lick. *I'll definitely be changing my panties after this meeting,* she thought. She was a visual person and right now the only thing she could visualize was seductively bouncing on top of him and riding him like the bull she'd ridden at her sister's bachelorette party.

"Is that okay with you, Ms. Rayne?" asked Mr. Vallant. *Crap, she'd missed the question.* "Yes, that's fine with me," she replied, hoping that her answer would suffice.

"Great. Ladies and gentlemen, that concludes our meeting. I'll see you all tonight at the reception."

Cyd quickly grabbed her belongings, politely smiling to the others as she tried to leave the room so she could seek refuge in the privacy of her hotel room, but Shawn had other plans.

"Are you ready?" Shawn asked, gently catching her arm before she dipped out into the hallway.

"For what?" she asked, trying not to notice his blatant appraisal of her outfit. He smelled of men's soap and aftershave that complemented his natural masculine scent. The fact that she could also detect that he was wearing a brand of Kenneth Cole's cologne to match the scent of aftershave both aggravated and aroused her at the same time. She'd never noticed those things about a man before, yet with Shawn she noticed every little detail. She nervously played with her hair, awaiting his response.

After one more look at her outfit, he finally decided to answer. "You agreed to let me take you on a tour of the building."

"No, I didn't."

"Yes, you did," he said, standing a little closer than before. "And you also agreed to let me escort you to your hotel to ensure that everything is well with your accommodations."

Cyd took a step back from him. "No. I. Didn't," she said a little slower than before. That was probably what Mr. Vallant meant when he'd asked her if she was okay with something. She just hadn't known what that something was until now.

"Look, Mr. Miles, I—" Cyd stopped talking when Shawn let out a hearty laugh.

"Mr. Miles? Seriously? After everything we've done, you want to be formal with me? Tell you what. How about you call me Mr. Miles when we're around everyone else. But when we're alone," he said, stepping back into her personal space, "I want you to call me Shawn just like I plan to call you Cydney."

Was that a request or an order? Cleary Shawn didn't know what type of woman she was. Cyd did *not* take orders from any man. "Listen, Mr. Miles. Had I known you worked for the Peter Vallant Company, I would have never…" Her words trailed off when he leaned in toward her ear.

"There is no way you wouldn't have been intimate with me, so save yourself the trouble and don't deny something you know was bound to happen, anyway."

Talk about cocky! He really thought he had her eating out of the palm of his hand. Although she was the first to admit that part was true, the fact that he wouldn't let her finish her statements was nerve racking.

"Tell you what," Cyd said, crossing her arms over her chest, not caring that his eyes followed her movement. "How about you be the good golden boy and tell Mr. Vallant that you showed me around the building and made sure my room was okay. In the meantime, I will head to my hotel *without you* and I'll make sure I have Mr. Vallant's assistant give me a tour some other time." With that she walked away, got on the elevator and hightailed it out of the Peter Vallant Company.

Only when she had paid the cab driver, checked into her hotel and settled into the confines of her luxury room did she absorb the situation. "For the next month or so I have to work with Shawn Miles," she said aloud.

A quick call to her sister in her cab ride to the hotel had eliminated the notion that Daman and her partners had known that Shawn worked for the Peter Vallant Company. Too bad Imani was laughing so hard that Cyd didn't have the chance to vent to her.

"Truly comical." She would be laughing at her situation, too, if she wasn't too busy freaking out. Cyd walked over to the floor-length mirror positioned on the wall to give herself a pep talk. "You can do this!" she chanted a couple times, taking deep breaths in between chants. "You're damn good at your job and you can definitely handle a man like Shawn Miles!"

But could she really? Could she handle a man who brought her to her knees with just one look? It may sound conceited but she didn't lust after men—men lusted after her! Yet somehow, Shawn had managed to make her crave his touch…and his touch only.

She cracked her neck as she placed her arms on each side of the mirror. "What I need to do is take control of the situation," she said, getting closer to her reflection.

"Why can't I enjoy Shawn while I'm on the tour? Participate in a little sweet seduction in between planning?" She was an adult after all, one who could enjoy sex with Shawn if she wanted to. Cyd always did as she pleased, but she was beginning to realize that there were some things she should have thought about before taking action. This definitely wasn't one of those times.

She sprinted to her suitcase and pulled out one of her grandmother's old diaries. When Faith "Gamine" Burrstone had passed away years ago, Cyd had been devastated. Her mother, Hope Burrstone-Rayne, could barely function after the loss. The entire family was shocked by Gamine's death, but luckily, Imani had stepped in and helped the family through the tragic time. While the death had affected Imani in ways she'd never admit, Cyd admired the strength that her sister had. The Burrstone clan was a loving, yet overwhelming, bunch at times. There were many reasons why Cyd was glad that her sister had found a man like Daman, the main reason being the fact that he helped Imani realize that she wasn't responsible for everyone's life.

Although they were sisters, she never did have the type of responsibility to the family that Imani did. But that didn't make things any less complicated for Cyd. Her role in the family was always a little more rebellious. She was the go-getter and adventure seeker. The one you ran to if you didn't need someone to bail you out of jail, but rather needed someone to sit in the jail cell beside you. Cyd had long ago decided to dance to the beat of her own drum rather than follow directions or fulfill obligations. As her mother affectionately told her, Cyd's antics oftentimes brought her parents to the brink of heart attacks. She had it all, brains and beauty. Class valedictorian, prom queen, and she was voted in high school most likely to run the world one day. She had a big heart and wasn't at all selfish, but she also didn't really care what people thought about her decisions. Men sometimes feared her confidence, falling into the friend category and staying there. And with each and every romantic downfall, she told each man the same thing: "I'm not the relationship type. I enjoy being single and free entirely too much to spend my days engrossed in a man. Trust me, you don't want to go there. But we can still be friends." To this day, her friends and family didn't understand how she convinced so many guys to actually agree to be friends with her. "What can I say… I have a gift," she'd often respond. But having that gift made the fact that she secretly longed for a storybook romance so out of character.

Lying on the bed, she propped herself up on her elbows and began flipping through pages of the diary. Gamine had left her a few things in her will, but the most important had been her diary collection. As soon as Cyd had dived into the pages, she became engrossed in the life of a woman she realized she hadn't really known. She knew Gamine the mother and grandmother, Gamine the community activist, Gamine the best friend to all who graced her presence. She even knew Gamine the romantic since her relationship with her grandfather, Edward Burrstone, had been one that everyone in the family had admired. What she hadn't expected to find in the diaries was a woman who understood her more than she thought. A woman who used to be just like Cyd when she was her age and a woman who'd dared to dream big and live on the edge.

Cyd's fingers graced the page of her favorite entry, written during a time in Gamine's life when she had first discovered true love. Cyd was never much of a reader, but she'd read Gamine's diaries so much that every crème page was curled at the corners and tea stains were evident on more than a few places.

"So romantic," she said aloud as she reread one of her favorite lines. She wanted to find her Mr. Right, which was the reasoning behind her creating her love-versus-lust lists. Gamine's diaries had opened up a side of Cyd that she'd often kept concealed…even from herself. Hidden in the pages of Gamine's deepest thoughts were feelings Cyd longed to experience. An escape into a world that showed her, although she was one of a kind, many women shared her thoughts and feelings of finding the perfect man. It may not fit the persona that people were used to when they thought of the infamous Cydney Rayne. But it was how she felt, nonetheless.

She turned on her back and closed the diary, holding it close to her chest. Once again, the pages had given her the answer she desired. Shawn may have more "I don't" traits from her list than "I do," but a girl had a right to have fun. Who knew what things she could learn about herself through a man like that. Even though he'd caught her off guard and put her in her place a couple times, she liked that he was aggressive and not afraid to take her head-on.

Cyd got off the bed and put the diary back in her bag before heading to the shower. "Shawn Miles, wait till you meet the likes of Cydney Rayne." And she was certain he wouldn't know what hit him.

Chapter 4

At thirty-two, Shawn had finally met his match. He'd finally met a woman he couldn't get out of his mind, although part of him refused to admit it.

There were over three hundred employees and friends present at the Peter Vallant Company appreciation tour kick-off reception but Cydney Rayne was not yet amongst the crowd. Shawn tried to will his head away from the ballroom entrance as he checked for her in a pool of new attendees who entered. Still no Cydney. He barely registered all the women openly checking him out as he greeted employees he'd recently met.

Shawn usually had no problem bedding one woman after another, but after he'd met Cydney eight months ago, he hadn't felt compelled to have sex with any other woman. And he'd received plenty of offers. *Cydney.* He'd thought about calling her by her nickname, Cyd, but Cydney rolled off his tongue with such ease that he had to use her full first name. Plus, from the brief moments he'd gotten to observe her with her family at the wedding, he noticed that everyone affectionately called her Cyd and she played into the darling role. But when he was with her, he didn't see anything darling about her. She was a unique treasure. But his definition of treasure definitely meant in the bedroom. When he was around her all he saw was fiery passion, pure lust…all woman.

You should stay away from her, he reminded himself. He shouldn't even flirt with her. *But since when did it hurt to do a little flirting?* The voices in his head were not cooperating with one another and he could only assume it was a matter of time before the lower half of his body started siding with the less logical part of his brain. Shawn made his way across the room to Mr. Vallant, who was conversing with a few executives.

"Hello, Shawn," Mr. Vallant said as Shawn approached the group.

"Hello, ladies and gentlemen," he greeted. Curt nods from the men and polite smiles from the women were exchanged. Within two minutes he stopped a nearby waiter to ask for tequila on the rocks. He needed a shot of something to get through this night, anything to help him deal with uneventful conversations amongst an uptight executive team who had nothing better to do than kiss Mr. Vallant's butt. He didn't know why the men looked so tense. He didn't want any of the women in the group. There was only one woman on his mind. Only one woman he wanted to devour…whole, if he could. A woman with a sexy smile, succulent lips and a behind that fit so perfectly in the palms of his hands you'd think her butt was created just for him.

"You okay?" asked Paul Jensen.

Deciding to forget about Cydney, he focused his attention back to the group in front of him. "I'm fine. Just wondering what's the score of the football game."

"Bears are winning for now," responded Brittany Higgins, taking a sip of her drink while gaping at Shawn over her glass. When she fully lifted her head, her eyes told it all. He could sense that she'd wanted him from their initial meeting, and now had no qualms about making that fact obvious.

I really don't need this right now. After all, he was here to do a job, and if the FBI's suspicions were right, a man who worked for the Peter Vallant Company, more than likely an executive team member, played a significant role in the case. The team had been trying to demolish a huge drug operation for years and had recently tracked a van that was dropping off boxes of cocaine. The van traced back to the Peter Vallant Company and a lead informed them that someone who had higher ranking in the company was a key element in the operation. Peter Vallant, longtime friend of Shawn's boss, Agent Larry Wolfe, had agreed to help find the culprit, but Shawn knew he and his team had to pay attention to details. He needed to do more than just catch the person responsible. He needed to uncover the entire operation.

Shawn had always been great at socializing and after analyzing the group and providing a few key comments, the group was warming up to him.

"Here you are, sir," said the white-gloved waiter as he delivered his tequila on a silver platter.

"Thank you," Shawn said, taking the glass and sipping the strong drink. The cool liquor slid down his throat and the hairs on the back of his neck stood on alert. Shawn looked at the glass, surprised by the sudden kick he felt after only one sip. He quickly took another, this time feeling a kick in the lower part of his body. He shuffled his feet, his pants suddenly feeling too tight around his groin. *Maybe I shouldn't have had tequila after all.* He was seconds away from disposing of the drink when he heard the voice of seduction.

"Good evening," Cydney said as she sashayed her way to the group. He should have known she had entered the room. His body never reacted that way to a few sips of his favorite drink. *Why did she have to dress so sexy?* Her deep magenta dress clung to her curves while her jet-black hair was pinned back on one side and played over her shoulders. She didn't need much makeup but the slight makeup she had worn looked flawless on her smooth, buttery complexion and accentuated her natural beauty.

She found a place in the group standing right across from him with a glass of wine in her hand. *Why did she do that?* Why had she chosen to stand right across from him? He now had nothing better to do than imagine her sprawled across his bed, waiting to be enraptured by his body. Who told her to come down in a dress so tantalizing he swore he could see every crevice of her body?

But he wasn't the only one who'd noticed Cydney. The other men in the circle were on full alert, cracking imprudent jokes that caused her to giggle in delight. And Jim Pearson was the worst. Everything he told her made her slightly throw her head back in laughter and place her arm on his shoulder. But make no mistake, Shawn saw her glance at him every time she opened her sweet pink lips to let the cool wine enter her mouth. He watched her tongue slip in and out as if savoring the flavor before taking another sip, her long eyelashes fluttering with each taste. She was baiting him. He knew it. An unfortunately, the lower part of his body knew it, too.

Down boy, he inwardly cautioned to his piece, knowing he could spring out at any second if he continued to watch Cydney drink her wine. She wasn't going to make his undercover job easy, and now that he knew what he was dealing with, he would spend the night regrouping and reminding himself how important this case was. But right now, he needed to escape from the ballroom and away from temptation.

"Excuse me for a moment," he said to the group as he walked toward the exit and glanced over at Micah Madden, his lead security officer, to signal that he was leaving the premises.

Once Shawn was in the hallway, he unbuttoned his suit jacket and breathed in a sigh of relief. He quickly walked down the hall and found a conference room. He tried the handle and was relieved to find the door open. He kept the lights off and escaped to a nearby window overlooking the nicely lit city. Shawn loved nighttime and he appreciated the solace of the unoccupied room with the only sounds coming from nearby traffic and trains. Dropping his head and closing his eyes, he placed his hands on each side of the counter, taking a moment to calm his body. Cydney had him on edge. Wasn't it less than a week ago that he'd had her pinned to the wall of a walk-in closet?

"Reminiscing about great sex is not helping," Shawn said aloud to himself just as he heard the conference door creak open.

He stepped back from the window and placed his hand in the back of his pants, clutching a small pistol he always kept on him. As the intruder peeked their head through the crack, he quickly released his hold.

"Shawn, are you in here?" Cydney's sugary voice filled the empty room. She couldn't see him in the dark corner, but he could see her from the light in the hall-way. For a few seconds, he thought about remaining quiet so she could leave, but decided to make his presence known.

"Yes, I'm here," he said, stepping back toward the window so the moonlight could shine on his face. As soon as Cydney entered the room and shut the door, Shawn knew he was in trouble. Even in the darkness he felt her get closer to him with each step she took. When she finally reached him, she stood there in observation, the moonlight caressing every part of her face.

"Why'd you leave?" she asked, her beauty catching him off guard even though he'd just seen her. Up close, he noticed all the little details about her that he hadn't noticed in the ballroom. Right then and there, Shawn knew hands down she was the most attractive woman he'd ever seen.

"Shawn? Why did you leave?" she asked again after several moments of silence. Shawn crossed his arms over his chest and raised his eyebrows at her question. There was no way she hadn't known why he left the ballroom.

"Really, Cydney," he finally replied. "By the way you were sipping that wine, you'd think you were purposely trying to seduce me."

She fringed a look of innocence as she shrugged her shoulders. "I don't know what you mean, Mr. Miles."

Unlike the terse way she'd said his name earlier that day, this time she said it in an alluring way that solidified his worries. *I should have kept silent,* he thought, referring to moments earlier when she'd asked if he was in the room. She took a step closer to him, her bold chestnut-brown eyes trapping his sea-blue ones in her sole captivity.

"Although I was surprised to see you in the meeting this morning, I must say that I do believe this is another sign," she said, playing with the collar of his suit jacket. Shawn kept his arms crossed for fear that if he uncrossed them, he'd have no choice but to kiss her senseless.

"I was surprised to see you, as well," he lied, hoping she believed him. She squinted her eyes together in disbelief before tilting her head to the side with a soft sigh. Then she looked up at him and smiled that smile he was becoming all too familiar with. "What is this a sign of?" Shawn asked, although he had a pretty good idea.

Cydney moistened her lips with her tongue before dragging his head closer to her mouth. He expected her to whisper something seductive or naughty in his ear. Instead, she gave his earlobe a quick lick before moving to his neck. He was pretty sure he had done this move on her a couple times already, but she was reversing the roles. Her sensual fragrance was mingling with her natural scent of arousal, further enticing his senses. The erotic aroma smelled like a combination of seductive slices of citrusy fruits and sweet wildflower honey. He couldn't help but uncross his arms and pull her closer to him. His hands ventured to her bottom and he palmed her cheeks as her mouth went to work on his neck. Her kisses were soft, light and wet. Her body was hot in his hands, proof that she was just as aroused as he was.

She stopped kissing his neck and gazed into his eyes. Her hands moved from their grip of his head and made their way to his chest, lingering on his dress shirt. "Another sign that our affair that should have been for one night only may not be so brief after all," she finally answered, lightly biting her bottom lip. She leaned closer to his face again, her breath fanning his lips. She didn't kiss him, though. Instead, she kept her face close to his and placed his right hand over her heart. The fast beats only stimulated him more and he was sure she could feel him jumping in his pants on full alert. But she didn't budge. And when she blinked, she did so slow and inviting.

"I'm going to head back to the party now," she said, gently pushing up from his chest while dropping her hands to her side. He didn't let her go right away as his left hand still palmed one of her back cheeks. Seconds later, Shawn let her escape his grasp. They stood there for one more moment, neither saying anything but letting their body language speak for itself. Then Cydney turned and exited the conference room door, briefly looking toward the dark corner Shawn was still standing in.

An hour later Shawn got to his hotel room and quickly discarded his tie and suit jacket. Pulling his dress shirt out of his pants, he plopped down on the bed and dragged his long fingers across his face. He suddenly felt sorry for any male who underestimated the determination of an irresistible woman. Cydney was a siren, a seductress with the grace of a cat, fortitude of a lion and craft of a fox. Blended together, those qualities equaled temptation at its finest. They were leaving for Springfield in a couple days, so Shawn had to focus on his duties and not stray from his goal. Fortunately, the case was so personal to him, he wasn't sure he even had a choice. Shawn knew all he had to do was remember that fateful day years ago and suddenly everything fell into perspective. It would take all of his willpower to treat Cydney like he treated the other Peter Vallant employees, but it was something he had to do. He would prevail in this case and finally close a chapter in his life whether his body agreed with him or not.

Chapter 5

"Ms. Rayne, here are the tablecloths you were looking for. And I also have the name tag you requested."

"Thank you, Verona," Cydney said to Mr. Vallant's assistant as she took the tablecloths out of her hands and clipped the name tag to her shirt. The first day of the two-day golf tournament in Springfield, Illinois, was going just as planned. The Springfield supporters of the Rebuild Your Community initiative were really impressed by the classiness of the event. Although Cyd had been receiving plenty of praise from the Peter Vallant employees present, she owed a huge thanks to the golf club and community volunteers who had helped make the tournament possible.

Even with the hustle and bustle of supporters, volunteers and staff, Cyd couldn't help but notice Shawn's every move. He was standing right outside one of the large enclosed tents, so focused, intently observing the entire tournament. Yes, he was the CISO, but something about him seemed a lot more serious than he had been when they first met in Anguilla. Maybe it was because he was vacationing then, whereas now he was on duty.

Ever since the night of the reception, he'd avoided her like the plague. *Looks like playboy is playing hard to get.* But why now? Why the sudden desire to give her the cold shoulder? She had to admit that she did enjoy playing a good game every now and then, but could he really ignore her after the moments they'd shared?

One of the volunteers suddenly tapped her on her shoulder, interrupting her scrutiny of Shawn. In addition to the tournament, the golf club had been kind enough to let them use the land usually designated for weddings for their activity. Cyd hastily put out a few more fires and turned her attention back to Shawn. But he had vacated the spot he'd been standing at moments before.

"Hello, Ms. Rayne," greeted Jim Pearson just as Cyd was about to venture outside the tent.

"Hello, Mr. Pearson. How are you today?"

"I'm doing great. And please call me Jim."

"Okay, Jim it is. You can call me Cydney if you'd like."

"I'd like that very much," Jim said, the look of flirtation marked in his eyes. "Might I add that you've done an excellent job with the tournament."

Cyd could tell he was interested in her. He'd sought her out several times during the kick-off reception. She could admit that he was really attractive. His blond hair and blue eyes were enough to make any woman swoon, but he just didn't do it for her. He didn't give her the butterflies that Shawn gave her. But since Shawn was ignoring her and Jim wasn't, she had no problem entertaining Jim's flirtation.

"Why, thank you, Jim. This tournament is just the start of many events to come for the appreciation tour."

He was watching her lips as she spoke and Cyd wished she felt even a little stimulation from the look, but she felt nothing.

"Cydney, I was hoping that you could go out to dinner with me tonight. I heard about this great seafood restaurant in the area. Would you be interested?"

Her first thought was that he didn't say her full first name as sexily as Shawn did. Her second thought was that she was going to turn him down gently and let him know she wasn't interested. But before she could say any of that, Shawn walked back into the tent and leaned on the edge of a table a few feet away from them. He didn't look too happy with her, or maybe he wasn't happy with the situation. Regardless, his presence changed the direction Cyd was originally going with her conversation with Jim.

"That sounds great, Jim! How about we meet in the lobby of the hotel 'round 6:30 p.m.?"

Jim's eyes lit up with excitement. "Sounds like a plan," he said, gently reaching out to touch her cheek. Cyd didn't like the gesture and on reflex, she sidestepped away from his touch. Unfortunately, it seemed to amuse him more than turn him off. When she glanced over at Shawn, his jaw was tight as if he was clenching his teeth. He'd crossed his arms over his chest and was glaring at her with obvious disapproval. *Serves him right for ignoring me.*

Turning her attention back to Jim, she gave him a polite smile before she told him that she had to check with the caterer before she continued setting up a few tables for lunch. When she walked out of the tent, she breathed in the fresh air and smiled to herself. "Doesn't feel too good to be ignored now, does it, Mr. Miles?"

she whispered to herself. "Ahh," Cyd said with a gasp when she felt a hand tighten on her arm before she was pulled behind the main golf club building away from the crowd.

"That's what you think I'm doing?" Shawn said as soon as they were alone. "Ignoring you?"

"What's with the tight tree grip, Tarzan?" Cyd said sarcastically as she yanked her arm out of his hold. "Don't you know it isn't nice to sneak up on people when they aren't paying attention?"

Shawn crossed his arms over his chest again. Didn't the man know how sexy he looked when he did that?

"Don't you know it isn't nice to gossip about people behind their backs?"

"I wasn't gossiping about you behind your back," Cyd said, taking a step back from his imperial stance. "Gossiping would imply that I was talking about you to someone else. Quite the contrary, Shawn, I was talking to myself." How dare he pull her behind the building like she was a child being scolded? "What are you really upset about? The fact that you overheard something you weren't supposed to hear or the fact that I was flirting with Jim Pearson?"

His jaw twitched at the mention of Jim's name. Cyd definitely wasn't romantically interested in Jim, but Shawn didn't have to know that. After he'd ignored her for the past few days, a little payback wouldn't hurt.

Shawn shuffled from one foot to the other, his eyes burning a hole through her. "Why don't you stop this whole…thing that you're doing," Cyd said, flaring her arms around his stance, referring to the way he was trying to intimidate her. She mimicked his posture by crossing her arms over her chest, as well.

"Is there something else you wanted with me?" The gleam in his eyes proved that he'd caught her double meaning and he let out a slight laugh.

"Woman, you are unbelievable," he said aloud, giving her another laugh. "I want a lot of things from you." He took another step closer to her and uncrossed his arms, placing one hand in his pocket while the other tilted the bottom of her chin toward his face and stayed there. "I have a job to do, just like you do. You can flirt with whomever you want to, but when you're finished entertaining Mr. All-American Boy, I'm sure you'll be seeking me out."

Cocky, cocky, cocky... Why the hell did he have to make cocky look so damn sexy! Cyd uncrossed her arms, lightly smacked his hand away from her chin and placed her hands on her hips. Evidently, Shawn was used to playing this hot-and-cold game with women. But she hadn't forgotten all the things he'd said to her at the wedding. He could pretend like he was unfazed, but they both knew better.

"Who do you think you're kidding? Quit acting like you aren't jealous of Jim. I saw you staring at him like you were ready to come over and pounce him to the ground." She adjusted her blouse and bra, knowing he would look at her breasts bounce into place after the adjustment. Just as she hoped, he took the bait. "I'm going out with Jim tonight, and who knows, he may just be the type of man I've been looking for."

Shawn let out a hearty laugh. "I doubt it." She didn't miss the flash of jealousy cross his face. As he turned and walked back to the crowd of attendees, Cyd rounded the corner and admired his powerful walk as he retreated back to the standing position he'd had earlier.

He looked too good in his casual black slacks and blue polo. Cyd sighed to herself as she thought about her date with Jim. She'd pick fighting with Shawn over flirting with Jim any day.

When Cyd and Jim arrived at the restaurant, Cyd was already dying to get back to the hotel. She couldn't stand a man who only talked about himself and his accomplishments and didn't give anyone else an opportunity to get a word into the conversation. Within the first two minutes of their being in the cab, she was bored out of her mind. Then they arrived to the restaurant and had a ten-minute wait, which usually wouldn't have bothered her. But since she had to sit there and listen to Jim talk about the time he thought he wanted to be a restaurant owner, those ten minutes felt like an hour. Now she had ordered her favorite seafood dish and was at this beautiful restaurant forcing herself to be entertained and failing miserably. Not that Jim even noticed her boredom. He was too busy talking about his days growing up in Omaha, Nebraska.

"Are you enjoying your dinner?" Jim asked. Cyd looked down at her plate that was almost completely full. He was making her lose her appetite.

"Ah, yes. I'm enjoying my dinner," she lied as she took a sip of the red wine she'd ordered when they first arrived to their table.

"Great," Jim said as he flipped his head to get a piece of fallen blond hair out of his face. Even that move annoyed her because he flashed his pearly whites after every hair flip. When his cell phone rang and he excused himself, Cyd welcomed the alone time.

She was finally able to finish her meal in his absence. After the waiter cleared their plates and placed the check on the table, Cyd looked around since Jim still hadn't returned. She spotted him through the window, standing outside in what looked to be a heated conversation with someone on the phone. Although she'd known him for less than a week, she hadn't seen him get aggravated or angry, but he was definitely angry now. She stood and walked to the window to try to wave him inside so they could pay for the bill and leave. When he finally noticed her, he held up his hand in an extremely rude fashion and started pacing back and forth.

Cyd was growing more annoyed by the second so the quicker she paid the bill, the better. After she settled the check, she walked outside, a little apprehensive to approach Jim. She decided to walk slower when she neared him so he wouldn't hear her heels click on the surface.

"I understand," she heard him yell to the person on the other end of the phone. "I've done everything you asked. Now I need you to listen to what I'm saying. I have a bad feeling about this and I think we should hold off until after the appreciation tour."

Cyd tried her best to tie together the bits and pieces she heard him say, but it wasn't making any sense. His pacing had quickened and he was continuously brushing his fingers through his hair. When she took another step closer to him, her heel clicked to the ground louder than she intended. Instantly, Jim lifted his head to her as he placed his hand over his cell phone receiver.

"Do you need anything?" he asked abruptly as if they hadn't originally been out on a date.

"Um, no," Cyd replied uncertainly. "I was just letting you know we can head back to the hotel."

"Please take a cab without me," Jim said very briskly and straightforwardly as he turned his back to her and continued his conversation, lowering his voice this time.

The nerve of that a-hole, Cyd thought to herself as she got into a cab that was waiting in front of the restaurant. *That man clearly has issues.*

Chapter 6

"Shawn, we need to see you in room C3," stated the voice on the other end of his earpiece.

"On my way," Shawn replied into his two-way radio microphone connected to the collar of his polo. Last night he'd followed Cyd and Jim to the restaurant and had been up later than he'd planned. Shawn had been surveying Jim Pearson since he'd begun his undercover work for the Peter Vallant Company, but besides a few fuming phone calls, he hadn't been able to catch anything else. Each time, Jim's call had been received from an untraceable number and the caller had hung up after a few seconds. But last night, Jim had stayed on the phone a little longer than expected. He was hoping Micah had been able to find something. Micah Madden, younger brother of his friend Malik Madden, had recently quit his job with Little Rock, Arkansas, P.D. after realizing the system was way more corrupt than he'd originally thought. Shawn had instantly told him about his goal to start his own company and Micah had jumped on the idea to help him.

When he reached C3, he swiped his key card to enter

the room. "What did you find out?" Shawn asked Micah as he entered and shut the door. He grabbed a nearby chair and plopped down at the desk that contained several laptops and various security devices.

"We traced that call to an abandoned warehouse thirty miles from here, right by the lake. I sent four members of the team to the location, but they didn't find anything. Whoever was there was long gone by the time we arrived."

"Do we know who the phone belongs to?"

"It's a disposable phone, but we're trying to run it through a number of databases now. My guess is that the phone was discarded into the lake."

"Did they find any prints?"

"No prints. This person was smart and did a good job covering their tracks. Luckily, they couldn't hide their tire tracks. Take a look at this," Micah said as he turned the computer so that Shawn could get a better look.

Shawn got closer to the screen and analyzed the tracks from the photo and video footage. They were too small to be a truck or a car. "So our mystery man rides a sports bike."

"Exactly," Micah said, snapping his fingers together. "Now all we need to do is figure out the make and model of the motorcycle. Could be a Ducati or a Kawasaki."

"Naw, the dirt lines from this baby are too smooth and precise for a Ducati or Kawasaki," Shawn replied as he pointed to the lines on the screen. "Looks like a BMW. Probably the K1600 series, but I'm not sure."

"How do you know?"

"Take a look at the tire indentation," Shawn said, actually touching the screen this time. "From the way the bike leans, it appears to have a narrower six-cylinder engine, like the BMW K1600 series. I did a lot of research when I was deciding on my motorcycle so I'm pretty familiar with sports bikes."

Shawn stood from his seat and leisurely placed both arms on the desk. "Have you found anything in the vans yet?"

"Not yet," Micah answered. "So far, Jim Pearson hasn't been anywhere near the vans since we started the investigation. No one from inside or outside the company has, with the exception of those who have clearance. And we've investigated all the drivers and employees who regularly use the vans, but they're all clean."

"Okay," Shawn replied as his forehead creased in thought. "Continue to monitor the vans. I need a few members of the team to head to Carbondale, Illinois, next week before the Peter Vallant Company arrives. The hotel has already been prepped so we have clearance to tap into their security cameras."

"I'll inform the men."

"Thanks. Did you hear anything from the private investigator?"

"They haven't found anything yet."

Shawn wasn't familiar with some of the newer members of the agency so he knew he needed to reach out to people he knew outside the agency if he was going to solve the case. "I need to make a few calls before the party tonight, including calling your brother," Shawn said as he stood to leave the room. "I also need you to head back to Chicago after we leave Carbondale to make sure we cover all of our bases." Micah nodded his head in understanding.

Jim Pearson was originally only appearing on two stops of the appreciation tour, but he had conveniently asked Mr. Vallant if he could attend all the events. After clearing it with Shawn and his team first, Mr. Vallant had obliged Jim's request.

As Shawn walked down the hallway toward his hotel room, he tried to shake the feeling in the pit of his stomach. Something just didn't sit right with him regarding the case. He knew as well as any law enforcement officer that sometimes the culprit was right in front of you, so Jim Pearson could definitely be their guy since he was the only executive team member who appeared to be into some shady side business. His demeanor during the investigation said as much. What he didn't know was whether Jim was the only Vallant employee who was involved in the drug case or if he was working with an accomplice outside of the company.

When Shawn reached his room, he went to the safe and took out all the paperwork he had on the case. Jim Pearson just didn't seem to have the mind-set of a criminal. He was guilty for sure, but was he the brains behind the transiting of the drugs?

As Shawn sat on the sofa and shuffled through stacks of paperwork, he thought back to that fateful day years ago when his life had changed. He'd been an FBI agent serving as a special deputy United States Marshal at the time. Not a day passed when he didn't wish he could rewind that entire day. So many more pertinent cases had surfaced since then, and FBI resources were needed elsewhere. But since that case was still open, Shawn was determined to do everything he could to find the person responsible. Although they'd captured Detroit's largest drug lord three years ago, the same marked drugs that were circulating through Detroit and Chicago back then were still circulating today. The DEA and P.D. in both cities were on the case, but Shawn needed to do more than solve the current drug situation. He needed answers that he'd been trying to get for the past three years.

He took out his Android and called his trusted friend and ex-FBI agent, private investigator Malik Madden. He answered on the first ring. "Hey, Malik, I need your help."

"Hey, man, what's up? Micah didn't mess up, did he?"

"Naw, man," Shawn said with a laugh. "You need to cool it on this big-brother kick. Micah's not that much younger than you." He heard Malik laugh. "I'm sending you a list of names that I need you to research as soon as you can. The FBI is coming up short and I think someone paid a lot of money to cover up their indiscretions."

"Say no more. Send me the list and give me at least a week, maybe two, to work with my connections." Malik was one of the FBI's finest and had been recruited while he was still attending Harvard University. But like Shawn, he'd always dreamed of operating his own business. After a little shy of ten years with the FBI, Malik had retired and opened his own private investigator firm.

"Thanks, man," Shawn said as he ended his call. "The FBI will do their research, and I'll do mine," Shawn said aloud before packing up his paperwork to begin getting ready for the party.

Once again, Shawn knew the exact moment that Cydney entered the banquet hall. He'd seen her hours prior directing the setup of the room and speaking with the banquet hall staff. When Shawn had originally seen Game Night: Come Represent Your Favorite Team! on the agenda, he hadn't known what to expect. Looking around at the pool tables, dartboards, mini basketball hoops, Ping-Pong tables and other games staggered around the large main room, he was greatly impressed. Cydney had managed to turn a sporting event into a classy production. There was even a section for hardcore casino players that included roulette and poker tables as well as several slot machines. Everyone had on their favorite jerseys, team T-shirts or hoodies, but no one looked as sexy as Cydney, who wore a clingy Bulls jersey. Shawn took another swig of his beer as he observed her outfit a little more closely. She'd tied a knot in the back, successfully showing off her amazing body shape. Her dark blue jeans hugged her apple behind in ways that made him jealous he wasn't denim material. When she bent over to pick up something she'd dropped on the floor, her shirt inched up, exposing the soft, creamy skin around her midriff.

"Can't take your eyes off her, right?" said a male voice standing behind Shawn. Shawn turned just as Paul Jensen was approaching him.

"Excuse me?" Shawn asked, pretending he didn't hear the question as he took another swig of his beer. Paul laughed as he shook the ice in his drink to break apart the cubes.

"Cydney Rayne? She looks damn good in that outfit, right?" Paul asked. "Although she looks great every time I see her."

Before he could stop himself, Shawn cut his eyes at Paul.

"Hey, man, I was just saying," Paul said, shrugging

his shoulders and laughing once again. *Keep your cool, Miles. She's not your woman.* Instead of responding he just smiled and initiated small talk about sports.

Ten minutes into their conversation, Brittany Higgins and Kim Lathers joined them.

"Hello, gentlemen," Brittany said, focusing all her attention on Shawn. While Kim led a conversation about the current status of the stock market, Brittany seductively sipped her wine, stealing glances at Shawn throughout the entire conversation. She was definitely an attractive woman and if Shawn wasn't so occupied with Cydney at the moment, he may have been inclined to return her flirtation.

"Shawn, what are your thoughts on the situation?" Brittany asked. Shawn didn't know if they were still talking about the stock market, or if they had moved on to another topic all together. He'd been too busy watching Cydney, who'd tried to watch their group discreetly ever since the women had joined them.

Shawn looked back at the group awaiting his response. "Ladies first," he said as he nodded his head toward Brittany, hoping she hadn't already answered.

"Oh, Shawn," Brittany said as she gently touched his arm. "You're too sweet." She tightly squeezed one of his muscles before she dropped her hand and answered the question, which luckily was still regarding the stock market.

As he pretended to listen to Brittany's response, he heard Micah's voice in his earpiece. "Jim Pearson has entered. East wing."

Shawn glanced discreetly at the east-wing entrance of the room in time to see Jim look around before his eyes landed fully on Cydney. Shawn wished the look he was giving her didn't aggravate him, but it did. Jim began making his way to her, but not before glancing over to where Shawn and the others stood. Jim's eyes zoned in on Paul and the two shared a look that didn't go unseen by Shawn. Both women had their backs turned to Jim, but there was no mistaking the contact between Jim and Paul.

Hmm. Interesting. Shawn was great at reading people, but he couldn't quite read the look on Paul's face. Was Paul involved in the transiting of drugs, as well? Was he the missing piece? Paul had never been on the FBI's radar, but then again, neither was Jim before Shawn began the investigation. A sideways glance at Micah proved that he was already taking note of both men's reactions to one another and had observed the exchange, as well.

Cyd straightened out the tablecloths draping the high tables as she tried to ignore the tinge of jealousy she felt. Watching Brittany Higgins flirt with Shawn was making her sick to her stomach. From where she was in the room, she couldn't tell if he was flirting back or not, but she was sure he was. What man wouldn't flirt with someone as attractive as Brittany? Cyd quickly glimpsed at the group again, just as Brittany laughed and flirtatiously leaned into Shawn.

Goodness, how tight is her jersey dress? Cyd thought. *Better yet, it looks like she just took a large jersey and tied it around her waist with a belt.* It didn't matter at that moment that she was just as guilty of wearing shirts as dresses just as tight, if not tighter herself. What did matter was that she hadn't foreseen

Brittany's interest in Shawn and chose to wear one of her scandalous dresses tonight.

"Cydney?" She turned around at the sound of her name and instantly wished she'd just ignored the person.

"Hello, Jim," she replied as she moved from straightening the tablecloths to fixing the centerpieces.

"I wanted to apologize for last night. I was extremely rude and I'm very embarrassed for the way the night went."

He's sorry? That's all he has to say after that hellish night? I'm sorry, too. Sorry for even going out with him in the first place.

"I understand," Cyd said politely. "I accept your apology." *Not!*

"Thank you," Jim replied. "I received an important phone call yesterday that needed my immediate attention. You know how it is when people want you to drop everything to help them…."

Cyd temporarily blocked him out as he went on another rampage about himself. Ever since Jim had arrived, Shawn had been looking her way a lot more.

"Am I right?" Jim asked, commanding her attention. She had no clue what he was talking about, but since it appeared she had Shawn's attention, she played into the doting-listener role.

"Yes, Jim," Cyd said with a slight giggle. "You are so right." She even playfully placed her hand on his shoulder, completely forgetting that she was supposed to despise him after the night from hell. She had to change their conversation to something even remotely interesting so she could keep playing her part.

"So why were you so angry on the phone yesterday?" Cyd asked, interrupting whatever he had previously been talking about.

"Just business," he said as he stuck his hands in his pockets. His jawline tightened and his eyes grew darker as if he were getting angry all over again. *Why the sudden change? He brought up yesterday first.*

"What kind of business?" Cyd asked. "Peter Vallant Company business?"

He shifted from the heels of his feet to the balls of his feet, his hands still in his pockets. He didn't answer right away so Cyd wasn't sure he'd heard the question. "What kind of bus—"

"Yeah, I heard you," he said gruffly, cutting her off. "I mean, yes, I heard you," Jim continued as he flipped his blond hair out of his face and flashed another all-teeth smile.

"Not Peter Vallant business, other business. I'm a man of many trades," he said, smiling once again. She wasn't sure if other women found his behavior attractive, but she definitely did not.

"Oh, really," Cyd said, ignoring his strange behavior. "Like what?"

He gave her a look that she couldn't quite read before answering, "Let's just say that my family is very wealthy and successful in the pharmaceutical business." By the way he responded, she assumed he thought she would be impressed. *Not likely,* she thought.

"That's nice," Cyd exclaimed. "Who owns the business?"

"Uh, my father does."

"Interesting. What's the name of the business?"

"Uh…it's Pearson Pharmaceuticals. I mean, Pearson and Company. I forgot they changed the name."

"Wow, interesting." *And by interesting I do mean the fact that you seem to be lying is what I find interesting.* "Why did they change the name?"

"You know, you sure do ask a lot of questions for someone who just met me."

Uh, DUH! That's typically what people do when they first meet.

"Just curious, I guess," she said instead. "I know people in that line of work. I was trying to figure out if we knew some of the same people."

"Babe, trust me. We don't know the same people," he said, as he stepped closer to her.

Cyd took it one step further and stepped even closer to him. "I'm not your babe," she said between her teeth as she tried to keep a smile on her face when all she really wanted to do was cringe.

"Not yet," he said, attempting to take another step toward her. Cyd stepped back before he got the chance. *Oh, man, he's so weird,* she thought as she observed his strange behavior.

"Okay, well, I have to get back to work," Cyd said as she turned to retreat to another part of the room. "I guess I'll see you around."

"Definitely," she heard him say after she had already turned her back to him. She went past the casino section of the room and out into a small hallway that led to the bathrooms. When she was alone, away from the crowd, she took out her iPhone and pulled up a Google web page to search Jim Pearson. Nothing popped up but the Peter Vallant Company website and articles associated with the company. Then she searched Jim Pearson, Omaha, Nebraska, after she remembered that was Jim's hometown. "Hmm, okay, that's strange," she said quietly to herself when nothing popped up in that Google search, either. She continued by typing in Pearson Pharmaceuticals in Omaha, Nebraska. Then she just typed in Pearson Pharmaceuticals. Followed by Pearson and Company. Zilch.

"So you're an ass and a liar," she quietly said aloud as she stuck her phone in the back pocket of her jeans. Since Shawn was ignoring her and she had two more cities of events before they returned to Chicago, she had to figure out what to do with her free time. The way she saw it, she only had one option. "Let's see who you and your family really are, Jim Pearson." Men lied to impress women all the time, but there was something about Jim Pearson that really got under her skin.

Chapter 7

Cyd dived into the hotel swimming pool and began doing laps. The day had been a long one, consisting of several family-oriented activities, relay races and many Halloween-themed events. Running after little children all day was exhausting and way beyond the duties of an event planner. She had so much built-up tension she could barely function.

It was day seven of her investigation on Jim Pearson and Cyd hadn't been able to track him down. *Why does he only bother me when I don't want to be bothered, yet when I'm trying to find him, he is nowhere to be found?* The Peter Vallant Company had arrived in Carbondale, Illinois, a couple days ago and Cyd hadn't seen Jim since they arrived, although he'd told her he would be here when they were still in Springfield.

Getting out of the pool, Cyd made her way to the whirlpool, anxious to relax after swimming several laps. She turned on the jets and submerged herself in the hot water, closing her eyes and soaking in the moment.

"Aah." She needed this. The water felt better than

she'd expected. She stretched out her legs and arched her back, preparing to take a quick nap in the water.

"May I join you?" she heard the deep voice say and prayed that she wasn't imagining him. Shawn hadn't been paying much attention to her since they'd started the tour so she knew it couldn't be him in the flesh, although she hoped it would be. She opened one eye first, expecting to see an empty space.

"Cydney..." He said her name breathlessly in a way she hadn't heard in weeks. She opened her other eye, taking in the complete sight of the man before her. She tried to speak, but she couldn't. His body had no business looking that magnificent. His swimming trunks were riding low on his hips. The indent of his pelvis bone was clearly visible. He'd grown a goatee that he hadn't originally had and goodness if that goatee didn't look sexy on him. His hair had grown out a little, too, so his fade was now a short crop of curls atop his head. She was taking too long to give him a response so he took it upon himself to get into the whirlpool with her. She felt like she was watching him in slow motion as he made the act of entering the water a truly provocative production.

When he was fully submerged in the water he looked up into the corner of the poolroom at the security camera before grabbing her waist and bringing her to the side of the pool not visible by the device. His back hit the opposite side of the whirlpool and she landed in between his legs, making a soft gasp when their bodies collided. He took one hand and tenderly brushed her wet hair out of her face.

"This is the other swimsuit you bought in Anguilla, right?" he asked as he played with the side of her purple bikini. It was getting harder for her to breathe under his unwavering stare. Although he looked sexier than ever, he also looked tired and a bit stressed.

So he sought me out instead of Brittany...interesting. Shawn and Brittany had been as thick as thieves lately and although Cyd tried not to be bothered by it, she was. But no matter how much Brittany flirted with Shawn and he flirted back, Cyd never saw him look at Brittany the way he looked at her. It was those moments that Cyd held on to.

"How did you know I bought this swimsuit in Anguilla?" she asked, finally finding her voice. Shawn gave her a killer smile before he answered.

"After I left the store that day, I watched you from the window to see if you would buy the other swimsuit I told you to purchase. I couldn't resist watching you."

Had any other man said those words to her, Cyd would have probably thought that it was creepy. But the fact that it was Shawn made her even wetter than the water they were immersed in. She leaned in a little closer and whispered into his mouth. "You watched me?" she asked.

"Yes," he said, his voice slightly cracking with desire.

"So you like watching me?" Cyd asked as she ran her fingers through his curls, breathing on his neck as she caressed his scalp.

"Yes," he said even deeper than before. His hands moved to cup her bottom, but she moved away from his grasp, careful to remember to stay out of the line of the camera. She leisurely untied the top of her bathing suit and placed the piece on the side of the whirlpool.

"What do you like watching me do?" she inquired

as she began to massage her breasts. The rise that she was getting from Shawn was motivating her to take her charade as far as he would let her. He hadn't answered her question, but it didn't matter. It was clear she had his undivided attention. She briefly turned to look at the poolroom entrance to make sure no one was entering.

"Don't worry. I locked the door," Shawn said, reading her thoughts.

"How did you get the key?"

"Don't worry about it," he said with a playful smile. She didn't really care how he got the key; she was just glad that the door was locked. She also didn't care that he had obviously planned to seduce her. Little did he know she had planned to seduce him first.

She continued her exploration of her breasts, massaging her nipples and throwing her head back in pleasure. The only way she could enjoy touching herself was if she imagined Shawn's hands caressing her instead of her own. So that was what she did. She imagined him caressing her…kissing her…licking her. Slowly, she rolled her tongue over her lips, softly moaning as she did. She brought her head back down and looked at Shawn. She hadn't seen when he'd removed his swimming trunks, but they were definitely discarded now and were lying by her swimsuit top. She stopped massaging her breasts and untied her bikini bottoms, throwing them by the rest of the wet clothes. Crossing one arm over her breasts, she took her free hand and allowed her fingers to glide up and down the side of her body, teasing him as he watched in anticipation and followed her hands to see where they would land. She reached out to flick a nipple at the same time she cupped her center, fully preparing to please herself and force him to watch. She didn't get very far because within seconds, Shawn had grabbed both of her arms, pulling her into his hold and onto his lap in the whirlpool.

"You are so naughty," he said right before his lips landed roughly on hers, his tongue enclosing over hers in his pursuit to make her pay for what she'd made him watch.

"I wasn't finished yet," she said in between his hungry kisses.

"You're finished," he stated in a fiery voice that confirmed he was done playing games. She'd successfully pushed him over the edge and didn't have any shame about it. He reached over to his trunks and pulled out a condom, his lips still plastered on hers. She lifted off his lap so that he could put on the condom and was in awe of how he continued to kiss all over her body and put on protection at the same time.

Seconds later, she climbed back on his lap and eased him inside her, clenching her vaginal muscles while he entered. The groan that escaped his mouth when he was completely embedded inside her was animallike. Gradually they began to move in a rhythm that was becoming all too familiar to them. Cyd rolled her head from side to side, overcome by the emotions shooting through her body as he cupped her butt cheeks and pumped inside her fervently. Thrust by thrust, he plunged inside, the tip of his manhood playing with the core of her essence every time he pulled out of her slender body.

"Cydney," he voiced on the brink of his orgasm.

"Me, too," she managed to say, her orgasm close to breaking free as a result of her body knowing his all too well. A few moments later, they both succumbed to their climaxes and experienced a feeling so powerful that the only thing they could do was hold on to each other tight and not let go.

What am I getting myself into? Shawn thought to himself for the umpteenth time as he walked down the hallway to the security room. He was in trouble. Big trouble. And it wasn't the kind of trouble he could talk his way out of. It was the kind of trouble that crept up on him quicker than he realized before he had time to truly react. Shawn wasn't even sure he could call it trouble. It was more like an obsession. He'd never been obsessed with anything in his life, not even solving the current case he was on that had ultimately changed his life. After years of thinking he was capable of solving any problem, he'd finally found a problem that he couldn't solve…and her name was Cydney Rayne.

Sex with a woman as gorgeous and intelligent as Cydney wouldn't normally be a problem for the average man. But Shawn wasn't an average man. His life wasn't an ordinary life and his past was far from normal. Therefore, Cydney Rayne was definitely a problem, and there was no doubt in Shawn's mind that he was, in fact, in big trouble. After their encounter in the poolroom yesterday, he'd successfully dodged Cydney any chance he got. She wasn't the type of woman to chase after a man, so one observation at his clear dismissal was enough motivation for her to ignore him, as well. But he hadn't missed the daggers she'd shot his way the night prior when he'd seen her in the hotel lobby. It didn't matter, though, because seeing her in another alluring dress had kept him up all night. She'd tiptoed into his mind, danced into his thoughts and hit him right where it hurt a man the most—his midsection.

"Shawn, Pearson has returned," Micah said as soon as Shawn entered the room. Shawn followed the direction of Micah's finger, which pointed to one of the mounted televisions streaming live security footage. The hotel had been extremely accommodating with his security team so they had been able to even place cameras outside of the hotel room Jim had been assigned to when he arrived.

"When did he get in?" Shawn asked, getting a little closer to the screen when Cydney's face came into view.

"Early this morning," Micah replied. "Nothing looked suspicious. Except…" His voice trailed off.

"Except what?" Shawn asked when Micah stopped talking midsentence. Micah shook his head and laughed, but still didn't continue.

"Except what?" Shawn asked again, growing slightly annoyed.

"I thought this was interesting," Micah finally answered as he reached for a remote and began rewinding the footage on the second television that was mounted on the wall. He slowed down the footage when he got to a part of the recording that showed Jim at Cydney's hotel room door before retreating to the elevator. Even in backward slow motion, Shawn was aggravated that Jim had been at her door.

"Just so you know, he followed her to her room. That's how he knew what floor she stayed on and her room number."

"What!" Shawn said a little more anxious than expected. He'd assumed she led him to her room.

"I figured you'd be pretty pissed when you found out."

Instead of responding to Micah, Shawn grabbed the

remote from him and began rewinding to the part when Jim started to follow Cydney to her room. Shawn balled his fists as he witnessed Jim intently observing her as she walked. It was either ball his fists or throw a punch at the television screen. He continued to watch as Cydney slid her key to open her door while Jim stood at the end of the hallway behind a large plant.

"That bastard," Shawn said aloud, not caring that he sounded like a jealous ex-boyfriend. Micah shook his head in pity. "Look, man, I don't know what's going on with you and Cydney Rayne, but I know that you need to get your head on straight. The FBI, DEA and P.D. are counting on you. Plus your company's on the line. You have a great team and she's a smart woman. Personally, I think she's just flirting with Jim to make you jealous."

Shawn cut his eyes at Micah. "Why do you think that?"

Micah laughed. "Um, I don't know. Could it be the fact that you have the hots for her? Or is it the fact that you can't seem to take your eyes off her anytime she's around? Or maybe it's the fact that you left me high and dry yesterday to sneak off and have sex with her in the poolroom?"

Shawn dropped his head back and dragged his hands over his face. "Crap. When did you know something was up?"

Micah looked at Shawn incredulously before he answered. "Are you serious, man? You know what, I'll pretend like you didn't just question my skills. You do a good job avoiding her so others may not know. But you don't pay me the big bucks to miss the obvious. After we solve this case, I think you'd better pick a location to headquarter our company and make me partner. You're reckless without me."

Micah slapped Shawn on the back as he finished reviewing the footage on the television. He laughed at his friend and soon-to-be partner because he was right. He was acting reckless, which was so out of character.

Before Shawn had even reached the poolroom yesterday, he'd known he was making a mistake. While he'd been reviewing the hotel's security cameras, he'd seen her enter the poolroom to take a swim. For a while, she'd walked around the edge of the pool in her cover-up and flip-flops as if she were contemplating between the pool and the whirlpool. When she'd decided on the pool, he watched her drop her cover-up, revealing a sexy bikini he'd recognized from their time in Anguilla. Within minutes, Shawn had given Micah an excuse about needing to relieve some stress and was out the door.

He'd questioned his motives up until the minute he opened the poolroom door and laid eyes on her in the whirlpool looking extremely sexy and appetizing.

"Shawn," Micah said, snapping a finger in front of his face. "Are you trying to figure out what Jim's doing with your woman or are you gonna sit there and daydream about her?"

Shawn gave Micah a blank look before grabbing the remote from him to rewind the recent footage. "So Paul Jensen showed up, as well?" Shawn asked Micah when he saw Paul flash across the screen.

"Yes. It looks like most of the executive board has been sporadically arriving."

"Interesting…. So they aren't following the schedule that Mr. Vallant created," Shawn stated rhetorically as he got closer to the screen and watched the way Paul and Jim glanced at each other. "Did they arrive at the same time?"

"Yes. About ten minutes apart."

Shawn glanced over at Micah. "We need to make sure we keep our eyes on Paul Jensen, too." Something was definitely going on between the two men.

Chapter 8

"Come on," Cydney whispered to herself. "Match point. Time to take him down." She straightened out her black tennis skirt before throwing the ball in the air and taking a swing. She wasn't a huge fan of tennis, but she was determined to show Jim Pearson her skills, anyway. When he'd asked her out for a game of tennis yesterday, she'd instantly declined his invitation despite the indoor tennis court being on the grounds of their hotel. Shawn's dismissal had really gotten to her. But upon remembering her investigation on Jim, she'd recanted her response and eagerly accepted his invitation. With the exception of a few chance meetings at the bar, they hadn't gone out on another date. Despite declining his previous invitations, she'd followed him on several occasions and had concluded that Jim was indeed keeping a secret.

"Yah," she yelled as she swatted the tennis ball. "Yah," she bellowed again, returning the ball and hitting it harder than before. Beads of sweat dripped from her forehead and her socks were slowly creeping deeper into her black-and-white shoes. She was, however, extremely competitive so she ignored her discomfort, determined to win the game.

"Yah!" She returned his ball with such force, Jim couldn't react fast enough, resulting in match point. Her win!

"Yay," she shouted as she placed her tennis racket under one arm while doing a fist pump in the air with the other arm. "Oh, yeah…oh, yeah," she said as she did a little happy dance, oblivious to the observant glances from neighboring tennis players. She stopped cheering when she noticed Jim's fixated stare.

"Okay, that was fun! Do you want to have lunch now?" Cydney asked. "I'll buy," she continued in a cute voice, swaying back and forth with a look of childlike innocence.

"Sure. Why not," Jim responded as he twirled his tennis racket in his hand in obvious frustration. For a brief second, he looked as if he wanted to throw the tennis racket into the wall, but that look left as quickly as it had come.

"Come on," she said as she made her way to him and linked her free arm through his. He reluctantly followed her down the hallway to a breakfast-and-lunch café. They were quickly seated and placed their order right away.

"So why weren't you on the tour for the past few days?" Cyd watched as he raised one eyebrow, undoubtedly taken off guard by her question.

"I had business to attend to," Jim responded drily as he played with his silverware on the table. He looked as if he didn't want anything to do with her at the moment, so Cyd was forced to try another tactic. She leaned over the table and gently placed her hand over his, twirling her fingers in a circular motion.

"I missed you a little when you were gone," she said, trying not to squirm as she voiced the words. She gave him a half smile, gently moistening her lips with her tongue. She had to remind herself not to go too far since Jim's personality had proved to be unpredictable.

He matched her movement and leaned into the table, as well. "How much did you miss me?" he asked as he made a smacking noise with his mouth as his tongue brushed over his teeth. He probably thought he sounded sexy, but the sound was both annoying and unattractive.

Cyd removed her hand from his, pushed her chair back from the table and crossed one leg over the other. "Oh, I missed you a lot," she continued with a laugh. "I realized that we never had a complete conversation. One of us always has to leave or work gets in the way."

"Really?" Jim said, clasping his hands together on the table. "You enjoy talking to me?"

Cyd contemplated her next words carefully. "I think there is a lot I don't know about you, Jim Pearson," she said as she let her voice drop a little lower. "And I definitely think there's more to you than what meets the eye."

His eyes lit up as if she'd said exactly what he'd been thinking. "That's so true," Jim stated, bringing his chair closer to the table. "All my life people haven't given me enough credit. I have a range of talents, but I hardly ever get credit for what I do!" His voice was rising as he talked.

Now we're getting somewhere.

"I understand completely," Cyd replied. "No one understands how talented you really are, Jim. Especially when it comes to handling business."

"Exactly," Jim exclaimed as he pointed at her as if she'd just pronounced a problem he'd been dealing with his entire life. "People underestimate me all the time. Especially when it comes to business. They need to realize that I'm an asset to this line of work and the sooner they realize that, the better it will be."

Cyd wondered what type of business he was referring to, considering he was the senior vice president of business development and had a large role in the company. She would understand more if he were the low man on the totem pole, but senior VP? It didn't make sense to her. *He must be talking about another type of business. Hmm...his family's business?*

"I agree. The sooner they realize, the better. Don't they understand that you could take over the business if you wanted to? Don't they realize your potential?"

Jim threw his hands up in the air. "That's what I've been trying to tell them for years. They just don't get it." Cyd observed his demeanor as his eyes squinted together in contemplation. "They really don't get it. After everything I've done and accomplished, disregarding the consequences, they still don't get it. Especially the one person who should."

"Exactly," Cyd added. "You're worth more than that."

"Damn straight," he said. "Especially when they are the reason I'm even in this line of work."

Her gut was telling her that the line of work he was referring to was definitely illegal. Cyd wanted to ask him who that person was, but she didn't want him to clam up if she pried too much. So instead she just sat quietly at the table and watched the range of emotions cross his face. Anger. Frustration. Revenge. And surprisingly, guilt.

She knew he was an intelligent man, but right now, he wasn't acting like a senior VP of a top real estate firm. He continued to talk, staggering his words as he spoke, nothing really making much sense. He would say some words in a higher tone, then he would lower his voice. Cyd had never met anyone who made her feel this uncomfortable. He wasn't directing any of his explicit words to her, but his behavior was unsettling nonetheless. She felt like she should stop their conversation, but instead she let him talk, unsure of what she would even say to him if she were able to get in a word. Luckily, their food arrived, causing him to stop his vocal rampage.

Jim looked down at his food, then back up at Cyd, coming out of his troubling trance. "This looks great," he said, his disturbing behavior suddenly stalled. Instead, his face instantly calmed and his frown was replaced with an award-winning smile.

What the hell? What was it with this guy? Cyd briefly contemplated distancing herself from Jim. But Shawn was still ignoring her so she didn't feel like she had much of a choice. She hated being bored, and at least focusing on Jim gave her a distraction. There was no doubt in her mind that Jim was a little dangerous, but he was an employee for the Peter Vallant Company so she didn't think he was a danger to her. As they began eating, once again, Jim began talking about himself.

"Tell me a little about yourself," Jim said, halfway through their meal. *Was he seriously asking about her?* He hadn't shown any interest in her personal life since they met.

"There's not much to tell," she replied, trying to keep the conversation impersonal. "As you know, I'm a co-owner of Elite Events, Incorporated and business is definitely booming."

"That's great," Jim said, taking a bite of his food. "What is your family like?" *Wow, he's two for two,* Cyd thought as she forked her salad.

"We're just a typical family," Cyd replied, minimizing the successes and accomplishments of her family. The Burrstone family was known for their many accomplishments in business ownership, community advocacy and entertainment. Usually, Cyd boasted about her family because she was so proud of everyone, but in this case, she appreciated the fact that she could withhold information because she had her father's last name—a name that had clout, but wasn't as well-known as her mother's family name of Burrstone. Besides, Jim didn't strike her as the type to research her on the internet. She turned the conversation back to him. "My family probably isn't as interesting as your family. I know people in the pharmaceutical business, but your family actually owns their business. What is your family like?"

The smile dropped from his face the instant she mentioned his family. He stopped eating his food and cracked his knuckles. "We aren't close. They've never accepted me and my decisions."

"I'm sorry," Cyd replied sympathetically. "Maybe they will come around someday."

"I doubt it, but it doesn't matter." Jim cracked his neck and resumed eating before he continued. "I have another family, so I don't need them or their judgment."

Cyd took a sip of her water. "That's good. What are they like?"

He didn't clam up as he had moments prior. But his current expression wasn't a pleasant one, either. He looked down at his plate. "They take me for granted, but they are a better family than my family ever was to me. I'd do anything for them."

"So when you were talking about your family earlier, you were referring to your other family? Why would you do anything for them if they don't appreciate you? That's not fair."

His face rose from his plate, void of expression. *Looks like I went too far.* He went from looking at her like a confidant to looking at her as if she were a threat to his "other" family.

"I'm done with lunch," Jim finally said as he waved over the waiter to get the check. Cyd looked down at her half-finished salad, forcing her eyes to stay down, avoiding Jim. He was still staring at her and even though there were other patrons in the café, the look in his eyes was a little intimidating. Cyd realized she was intimidated because he was void of emotion. She was pretty sure she had irritated him by asking so many questions and he was finally realizing how much he'd told her.

When they left the café, Cyd excused herself by saying she had to change before tonight's festivities began. They were headed to Indianapolis in the morning, so it was their last night in Carbondale.

"I'll see you later," Jim said, stopping her in her tracks. She turned back toward him and noticed his relaxed smile. The smile was even eerier than his being angry with her. Cyd gave a quick head nod and hurried away from him.

As she walked farther down the hallway, she couldn't

help but turn around to see if he was watching her. Surely enough, his eyes were glued in her direction.

Cyd opened a large manila envelope and poured the contents on the bed in her hotel room. She glanced at the array of pictures and notes she'd accumulated since she'd started investigating Jim. She found out a lot of valuable information at her tennis date with Jim earlier that day. She also realized that she needed to leave this situation alone.

Growing up, Cyd was always a bit of a detective. She loved the idea of solving the case of a missing sock or having a Q&A with her cousins on who ate the cookies from the cookie jar. She even entertained the idea of being a detective or investigator while she was in college, but she quickly realized that planning events was definitely her passion. When she was younger, her spy antics hadn't put her in any danger. Now she wasn't so sure. Although she didn't think Jim was really dangerous, she knew it wasn't smart to continue to investigate him. She honestly had no idea why she'd thought it would be a great idea in the first place. *Because you needed to occupy your time and get attention from someone else since Shawn was ignoring you.* The voice inside her head was right. Even though she disliked Jim to some extent, she did like the attention he was giving her.

Shawn. His named crawled into her mind for the first time all day. Shawn was the chief information security officer, so it only made sense for her to tell him about the suspicions she had about Jim.

"But how would I explain why I started following him in the first place?" she asked aloud. How was she supposed to explain to him that since he was ignoring her, she was bored and liked the attention she was receiving from Jim? She wouldn't dare give him the satisfaction of knowing how badly his dismissal affected her.

"But what other choice do I have?" She glanced at the pictures and notes again. Jim talked on the phone four times a day at precisely the same time every day. Twice, she'd noticed that the call came up unknown, which wouldn't seem like an issue except for the fact that he always seemed to leave her abruptly and answer like he knew the person. Her conversation with Jim today was icing on the cake.

Cyd began placing the pictures and notes back into the large envelope. "You have to tell him," she said to herself as she put on her gym shoes and texted Shawn to meet her in the lobby. She left her hotel room and headed to the elevator. As soon as the elevator door opened, out stepped Jim, running right into her.

"Oh, sorry," Jim said as he gripped her arms to help her maintain her balance.

"That's okay," Cyd said, slowly easing herself out of his grip. "Why were you walking so fast, anyway?"

"I guess I was just anxious to see you," he said, although Cyd didn't believe him. She straightened out her T-shirt and yoga pants, making sure she tightly gripped the envelope, holding it close to her chest.

"I have to meet with the hotel staff before I finish getting dressed," she said, thinking quickly. She tried to move around him to get on the elevator, but he stepped in front of her. "Do you have to leave right now?" Jim asked as he bent down to tie his shoelace while stationed in between the elevator and floor. "I was hoping we could have a little wine before the events later today."

Only then did Cyd notice the wine bottle and glasses in a tote bag on the floor of the elevator.

"Sorry," Cyd exclaimed as she finally made it around him and into the elevator. "I have a lot to do tonight and before we get to Indianapolis. Can I take a rain check?"

Jim stood there for a few seconds and Cyd prayed he wouldn't give her a hard time. "That's fine," he finally said as he stepped back into the elevator with her and pressed his floor number.

"Great," Cyd exclaimed in relief. After Jim got off on his floor and the elevator let her off on the ground level, she spotted Shawn waiting in a corner of the lobby. His head immediately turned as she approached him.

"Hello, Shawn." He had on a pair of worn jeans and T-shirt. On any other man, the outfit would look casual, but on Shawn, it looked rugged and sexy.

"Hello, Cydney," he responded in his raspy voice. "What did you want to talk to me about?"

Cyd glanced around and pointed in the opposite corner of the lobby that had a couple chairs and a table. "Do you mind if we sit over there?"

"Sure, why not," Shawn said as he followed the direction of her hand. When they arrived at the chairs, taking seats right across from each other, Cyd opened the manila folder, but didn't remove any contents. "I wanted to talk to you about an employee who I believe may be up to something."

Shawn's eyes squinted together as he placed his forearms on his knees and clasped his hands together. "I'm listening," he said, giving her the green light to continue.

Cyd explained the entire story, leaving out the part about her wanting attention from Jim due to Shawn's decision to ignore her. The corner they were stationed at was very private, so Shawn was able to unobtrusively skim through the pictures and notes without looking suspicious.

"So you've been following him?" Shawn asked, although the question had to be rhetorical since she'd already told him that. "Why did you think that was a good idea? Do you know how much danger you put yourself in?"

Cyd was taken aback by the way he was speaking to her. She felt much younger than her twenty-seven years. "Seriously, I'm an adult, so I'd appreciate it if you talked to me as such."

Shawn threw his head back in a sarcastic laugh before leaning over to talk lower. "For an adult, you certainly weren't thinking like one when you created a plan to investigate Jim Pearson." He leaned even closer to her. "Cydney, I will look into this. But I need you to stand down and drop this investigation. You're liable to get hurt."

She wished his concern warmed her heart. Instead, she was irritated and a little embarrassed that he thought her investigation was so childish. She'd wanted to tell him because she'd known it was the right thing to do. What she hadn't planned on happening was her feeling stupid for even coming to him in the first place. When she'd first met him in Anguilla, she'd felt a passion unlike any she'd ever experienced. When she'd seen him again at her sister's wedding, she'd felt desire at the highest peak. Ever since she saw him in the conference room, he'd made her feel minuscule and unimportant, with the exception of their time in the whirlpool.

"I understand," Cyd exclaimed, her voice rising

slightly. "I was only trying to…" Her voice trailed off as she noticed the look of irritation in his eyes.

"I know what you were trying to do," Shawn said in impatience. "I can't believe you'd be so irresponsible and put yourself in danger. I'll handle it from here."

His heartless words were like daggers to her pride and self-esteem, making it impossible for her to hold in her feelings.

"Well," Cyd said as she stood to retreat back to her hotel room. "Thank you, Shawn." She counted to three to try to get her emotions under control. "I hadn't known what rejection and humiliation felt like until I met you. But somehow you've made me feel both in a matter of weeks."

"Cydney," he said, standing and reaching for her.

"Don't touch me," she all but yelled as she moved away from his hands. She then brought her voice back down to a normal level. "I gave you control when I let you use my body in ways I'd never allowed any man." She got the courage to look him straight in the eye before she brought her lips to his ear. "Rest assured, Shawn Miles, I will *never* make that mistake again."

Chapter 9

"You're an idiot," Shawn said aloud to himself as he walked around the outside premises of the host hotel for the Indianapolis Customer Appreciation Cultural Fair. Yesterday, Shawn and Cydney had been placed on the same bus on their commute from Carbondale, Illinois, to Indianapolis, Indiana. He'd tried to talk to her several times and apologize, but each and every time he was rejected.

You deserve it after talking to her the way that you did, he thought to himself. Even worse, he should have been happy that she was just following Jim and wasn't actually attracted to him. He'd been following them both and had been unsure if Cyd was using Jim or if she actually enjoyed Jim's company. Shawn hadn't known what had come over him that day. He'd had a feeling that she was going to talk to him about Jim, but instead of being understanding, he'd reprimanded her as if she was a child.

Early this morning, he'd called Micah and told him there had been a change of plans and he needed him to reroute and meet him in Indianapolis. Micah was due to arrive soon and Shawn needed to debrief him on his recent findings. It was actually more like Cydney's recent findings. She'd gotten close enough to Jim to have some intimate conversations with him and the information she'd found out had given Shawn an idea.

"Man, what are you doing out here?" Micah asked as he approached Shawn. "I know it's still fall, but it's a little chilly."

"I guess I don't feel anything," Shawn said as he led Micah through a gathering of trees near a creek. He handed Micah a flash drive. "I scanned and uploaded all the files I received from Cydney. I need you to go through them while I prepare the team for the cultural fair that's starting in a couple hours."

"No problem." Micah placed the flash drive in his pocket.

"Great. I need to call Malik and see if he has an update."

"I talked to him on my drive over here. He wants to verify some of his findings, but he expects to give us an update tonight or tomorrow."

"That's perfect. After reviewing everything that Cydney found out, I think that Jim may be hiding more than we thought. For starters, there's no way Jim Pearson is in this alone."

"I thought the same thing weeks ago," Micah added. "He didn't go under the FBI's radar without any help from the inside."

Shawn was about to respond to Micah's statement when he noticed they were being watched from the window. "Did Malik tell you anything about Paul Jensen?" Shawn asked.

"Malik said he's clear. There's nothing in his background that would indicate otherwise."

"Well, he's definitely watching us right now from the window. Something about him doesn't sit well with me."

"Me, neither," Micah added, knowing he couldn't turn around to take a look. "Let's wait and see what Malik has found before we count him out."

"Definitely," Shawn agreed as he watched Paul leave the window. "Let's get to work," he continued as he began making his way back inside the hotel.

As soon as they entered through a side door near the lobby, Shawn wished he had stayed outside for a few more minutes.

"Shawn, there you are," Brittany said, briskly walking toward him.

"I'll go play catch up and review the files," Micah whispered in Shawn's ear before patting him on his shoulder and turning to leave.

"Hello, Brittany," he said when she grew nearer.

"Hey, yourself," she replied when she reached him. She looked attractive in her snug-fitting skirt and blouse, but she didn't make his body feel any bit the way it felt when he was around Cydney.

"So what time are you heading to the conference room for the festivities?" she asked as she played with the collar of his shirt. His eyes trailed from her manicured hand to her heavily made-up face. Despite her being attractive, he never did go for the prima-donna type. *I really don't need this right now.*

"Probably in a couple hours," he stated, making sure he looked her in the eye even though she'd perked out her chest, hoping he'd sneak a peek. "But I'll be on duty."

She closed the small gap between them and puckered her lips in a pout. "Not if I have anything to say about it." He had enough on his plate tonight and entertaining Brittany wasn't on his agenda at all. He noticed someone in his peripheral vision and slightly turned his head to get a better look, hoping it wasn't who he thought it was.

When his eyes landed on Cydney, she quickly turned her back to them but she wasn't quick enough. He'd seen the look of hurt on her face. Brittany noticed his attention was projected elsewhere and turned toward the direction of his gaze.

"I swear that woman spends too much time looking at you. Hasn't she gotten the hint already? You ignore her every chance you get." Brittany placed her hands on both sides of his collar and pulled him closer to her. "You'd think she'd save herself the embarrassment." She voiced the last statement a little louder than the others. Without turning around, Cydney walked out of the lobby, clearly having overheard some of the conversation.

Shawn grabbed both of Brittany's wrists and pulled her hands away from him. "I don't know what you're talking about, but I suggest you keep your mouth out of things you know nothing about."

"Ooh, so now you're done with me and you're all over Little Miss Perfect, huh?" Brittany flipped her weave over her shoulder. "It's cool, though. Just wait until you see my dress tonight. You won't even be thinking about her. You'll only see me."

Was she delusional? How did I even get myself wrapped up in a love triangle? Shawn knew whatever he said would only make the situation worse, so he excused himself and went to the security room, glad to find Micah in there reviewing the documents he'd received from Cydney.

"That woman is crazy," Shawn said as soon as he closed the door and took a seat next to Micah.

"I can tell that much from the little episode that just happened in the lobby," Micah said with a laugh as he pointed to the television screen with the camera aimed at the exact spot Shawn and Brittany had been standing. "Man, you've got these women all over you."

"I guess so," Shawn responded. "Why me and not you, I have absolutely no idea."

"Me, neither," Micah said with another chuckle. "I'm younger and more attractive."

"You may be younger, but you wish you looked as good as I do," Shawn laughed. "Okay, on to more important matters," he said, quickly changing the subject. "I spoke with Agent Wolfe and Mr. Vallant to update them on our progress. Mr. Vallant will actually arrive in thirty minutes. How much did you cross-reference between our footage and Cydney's?"

"Enough to know we need to regroup and call all the men together before tonight's cultural fair. My gut is telling me we need to be on alert tonight."

Shawn had the same feeling in the pit of his stomach. "My sentiments exactly."

The cultural fair cocktail hour had begun thirty minutes ago and so far, everything was running smoothly. The Peter Vallant Company had several rebuilding initiatives in the Middle East and Africa, most of the contributors and investors coming from Indianapolis and Chicago. Mr. Vallant had arrived and uttered his appreciation for all of their hard work so far and the attendees really seemed to be enjoying the worldly theme in dedication to the different countries they'd helped.

Cyd looked down at her iPhone when she heard it ding, indicating that she had a text message. The cultural event in Indianapolis and the formal ball in Chicago were the two large events she had planned that required her to have contact information for the entire executive staff in case someone who was scheduled to give a speech couldn't attend. Unfortunately, that meant that she had to give them her contact information as well, which included Jim Pearson. Though up until now, he hadn't texted her.

In case you are looking for me, I had to step out for a minute. I'll be back in time for my speech to the attendees.

"Of course he had to step out," Cyd said aloud to herself. She just texted him a simple "okay" and got back to working the event. She wasn't going to concern herself with Jim anymore. It was too stressful and there was no doubt that Shawn would be watching her every move now. He'd been watching her from the minute she arrived in the hallway connecting all the conference rooms, his eyes glossing over her attire, fixating on the curve of her hips that graciously filled the beautiful black-and-teal African-themed dress she'd chosen to wear.

After seeing Shawn with Brittany, Cyd had given herself a pep talk before she'd left her hotel room. She was worth more than a man who only wanted her on his time and treated her as if she was a child instead of a grown woman. She'd expected them to have a respectful conversation, but all she'd gotten was an unpleasant lecture. *Maybe I needed him to act that way so that I could work him out of my system?* She realized when she'd decided to seduce him that he wasn't her Mr. Right, so in all honesty, she shouldn't even be angry at his behavior toward her.

But he seems so different than that man I met in Anguilla. She couldn't get over the fact that he seemed so infatuated with her one minute, yet the next, he could flirt with another woman right in her face.

"Ms. Rayne, everyone is gathering in conference room A for the kick-off speech for tonight's events."

"Thank you, Verona," Cyd replied. When she arrived at the conference room, Jim was nowhere in sight. Mr. Vallant was giving the kick-off speech, which meant Jim was the next executive member to speak.

"Kim," Cyd said as she approached the CMO. "Can you say a few words before Jim?"

"Sure thing."

"Thanks so much," Cyd responded as she made her way through the crowd to find Jim. Shawn's right-hand man was standing near Mr. Vallant. She briefly looked around for Shawn so she could tell him she was going to search for Jim, but decided against it when she noticed Brittany twirling in front of him in a dress so tight, Cyd could see the imprint of her thong.

"Forget this," Cyd said to herself as she also dismissed the idea of telling another member of Shawn's team. She made her way to the elevator and pressed the floor number that she'd seen Jim press when they were in the elevator together. She didn't even know what room he was in, but she hoped she would run into him in the hallway, unless he'd left the building.

She stepped off the elevator and looked down both ways of the hallway. After she didn't see anyone, she briefly placed her ear to each door she passed, hoping that he would be on a phone call so she could hear his voice. When she neared a room at the end of the hall, she placed her ear on the door and it pushed open. She looked at the cracked door and contemplated her next move.

"Jim, are you in here?" she asked as she clicked on the light and pushed the door open a little more. No answer. She stepped into the entryway. "Jim?" she called again, in case he was in the bathroom. Still nothing. The room looked spotless...even cleaner than it would be after housekeeping. Cyd dragged a nearby potted plant to the door to keep it propped open before she walked completely into the room. It was the same size as her suite, only everything was on the opposite side. She checked in the bathroom and closet with no sign of Jim. As she got closer to the coffee table, she turned on a lamp to see if there was any sign that this was Jim's room. She noticed a thermos with the initials J.P. etched on the side sitting on the table. Jim usually carried the thermos to all the hotel breakfast buffets every morning and filled it with coffee, so she was confident this was indeed his room.

Right next to the thermos was a small heap of documents. The contents spread out on the table stopped her in her tracks. She picked up a few pictures and notes that were paper clipped together. Removing the paper clip, she shuffled through the documents.

"Oh, no," she said when she noticed they were the

pictures and notes that she had taken of Jim. Racking her brain, she remembered when she'd bumped into Jim on the elevator. At the time, she hadn't thought she'd dropped anything. Then she remembered that he had stepped out of the elevator when he hadn't needed to and stepped back in before it closed. *Had he pushed the pictures into hiding when I ran into him?* She suddenly dropped the pictures on the table when she noticed a picture of herself clipped to a file folder. The picture was taken the day she'd arrived at the Peter Vallant Company.

Her fingers were trembling as she flipped open the folder and spotted several more pictures of herself and a timeline of her daily schedule since the start of the appreciation tour in Springfield, Illinois. When she left for her morning jog and the time she had lunch every day. But then she noticed more pictures in the back of the file that included her life before the appreciation tour. Jim had pictures of her leaving a clothing store and walking out of Union Station in Chicago. Cyd brought one hand to her mouth to cover her gasp as she noticed more personal pictures of her walking down the street to work and others of her leaving her condo. And another when she entered her condo's parking garage to get to her car. She looked at her outfits she wore in the pictures and realized they were all taken after her first meeting at the Peter Vallant Company months prior.

"Oh…my…God," she said, dropping all the contents in her hand as they landed on the table and partially on the floor. *How could I not notice I was being followed,* she thought. She became instantly overwhelmed by the information she'd just uncovered, and Shawn's cautionary words that she had put herself in danger popped into her mind.

She lifted her head as her heartbeat quickened. He was there…with her in the room. He had to be. It felt like a setup and she was pretty sure she'd fallen right into his trap. She lifted her head and noticed a shoe sticking out from under the curtain in her peripheral vision.

The best thing you can do is pretend you didn't see his shoe and make a run for it, she thought to herself as she tried to slow down her heartbeat. Within seconds, she leaped over the table and ran toward the door. One more leap over a plant and her right arm and leg were already out the door. But he was quick on her tail and caught her left arm and placed his leg in front of her left one.

"It's about time you found out my secret," Jim said to her as he pulled her into his chest and kicked the plant that was propping the door open out of the way.

Cyd screamed, but Jim placed his hand over her mouth as his arms pressed into her abdomen. She chose not to say anything else for fear that her mouth over the past few weeks had already gotten her in enough trouble. He brushed her hair out of her face and pulled a handful to his nose.

"I always loved how your hair smelled," he said to her as he pulled her unwillingly to the balcony. He opened the door and dropped two rope ladders over the railing. "It's time for us to take a little trip," he said before he told her to remove her heels and climb down the ladder.

"In case you think about pulling any funny business, this should help diminish those ideas." Cyd felt the cold handgun pressed against her side and she nodded in understanding. *Oh, no…. What have I gotten myself into?*

Chapter 10

Something isn't right, Shawn thought as he dodged around Brittany, who had been flaunting her outfit in front of him since she'd arrived. He glanced at Kim Lathers as she was concluding her speech before he opened the agenda and noticed that Jim Pearson had actually been supposed to speak before her. He could barely hear himself think over the flirtatious words Brittany was throwing his way.

"Brittany, my apologies, but I'm definitely *not* interested. Why don't you find another man to intrigue," Shawn said as he gently pushed her away from him. She muffled an expletive under her breath before flipping her hair over her shoulder and sauntering away from him.

"Any visual on Cydney Rayne or Jim Pearson?" Shawn said silently into the two-way radio microphone. The voices on the other end of his earpiece all voiced no. Micah got offstage and headed over toward Shawn. "Paul Jensen is toward the front of the audience, but no sign of Jim."

"Or Cydney," Shawn said, moving across the crowd.

He gave his men orders to be on alert while he and Micah left the room.

"I'll check Jim's room and you check the security cameras," Shawn said to Micah.

"Right away," Micah replied before running down the hall to the security room. Shawn took the stairs in hopes that he would find Jim or Cydney in the stairwell. No such luck. When he reached Jim's floor, he pulled out his pistol before opening the door to the floor.

The level was quiet and as Shawn made his way to Jim's door, he hoped that his suspicions weren't true. When he reached the door, he opened his wallet and took out a credit card. He entered his room key card into the slot, knowing it wouldn't unlock the door, but needing it to at least prompt the process of recognizing if the key was correct so he could slide his credit card into the side of the door at the same time. After three tries, it worked and the door popped open. Shawn did a quick, yet thorough, scan of the suite and concluded that neither Jim nor Cydney were in the room.

"Shawn," Micah called into his earpiece. "The cameras show Cydney entering the room that had been left open and not exiting. It's hard to say, but I think she tried to get out because five minutes later, there appears to be an arm that reached out of the door before the door closed."

"Crap," Shawn voiced into his two-way mike as Micah confirmed his suspicions in the same moment that he noticed pictures of Cydney spread out across a coffee table. Shawn saw the window curtains sway as a soft breeze floated into the room.

"Micah, he's got her and apparently he's been following her since before the tour," Shawn said as he ran to the balcony, immediately noticing rope ladders hanging over the edge. "Check the outside security cameras. Men, one of you is to stay alert in conference room A while the other two check the lobby and inside the hotel."

Shawn placed both arms over the balcony and scanned the grounds below, trying to find anything in the darkness. He noticed a couple walking in the distance and knew from the way the woman walked that it was Cydney and Jim. Since she wasn't screaming, Jim had to have a gun.

"Men, they're outside in the south wing." Without giving it a second thought, Shawn leaped over the balcony and began climbing down one of the ladders.

"The speeches have concluded in conference room A," voiced one of his men. "But I noticed a few extra men that hadn't been present the entire night."

Shawn's hands tensed on the rope as he listened to one of his men request that the other two stay alert in the hallway. Now that the kick-off meeting had concluded, it was harder to keep eyes on everyone. Shawn waited until he was on ground level before speaking into his microphone again. "I need someone here to assist me in the south wing. Pearson is in sight."

"I'll be right there," replied one of his men.

If Shawn knew anything, he knew that he didn't have time to wait for help to arrive. There was no way he was letting anything happen to Cydney. Shawn reached them in record time and hid behind a bush to see why Jim had stopped walking. Then he noticed the parked van covered by tree branches. It looked just like the Peter Vallant Company brown vans but a glance at the number on the side of the van proved that it wasn't one of the originals. *He duplicated the van,* Shawn thought as a few other pieces of the case began melding together. There was no telling how many had been duplicated.

Shawn got a little closer to them when he saw Jim place his gun on the top of the van and dig in his pocket to answer his phone. From Shawn's angle, he saw Cydney glance around the area as if contemplating what her next move would be. *She probably knew the call was coming,* Shawn thought as he remembered the personal investigation Cydney had conducted. Jim yelled into the phone, distracted by the caller and in obvious disagreement with the plan the caller must have stated. Jim's distraction gave Shawn his opening to rescue Cydney.

He quietly approached Jim and Cydney, only pressing his pistol to Jim's back when he heard him end his phone call.

"I suggest you don't make any sudden movements," Shawn said as he used his other hand to knock Jim's gun off to the other side of the van. "Now release your hold on Cydney."

Jim did as he was told, and as soon as he did so, Shawn pushed Jim against the car before turning him around and securing his arm under Jim's neck.

"Shawny boy, you're way out of your league with this," Jim said in a strained voice when his eyes landed on Shawn.

"We'll see about that," Shawn said as he pushed his arm farther into Jim's neck and took out his handcuffs.

"You're right," Jim said with a vindictive laugh. "We will see. We'll see how macho you are when they get a hold of your stuck-up princess over there," Jim yelled as Shawn pushed his head farther into the van, after the handcuffs were secure. "You'd better watch your back,

Ms. Rayne," he added with a malicious laugh. Shawn roughly took him off the van and prepared to walk him toward the hotel, but Jim lunged toward Cydney as if to scare her more than he already had.

Thinking out of anger and pure irritation, Shawn bashed Jim's head against the door of the van and knocked him unconscious. He picked up his lifeless body and turned him on his back. Shawn looked up at Cydney, barely able to see her in the darkness.

"Cydney," Shawn called aloud. "I know you're angry and scared, but I need you to help me." She got closer to him and only then did he notice the unshed tears in her eyes. She looked down at Jim before squatting to help Shawn. Together, they pulled Jim's body a few feet as one of Shawn's men appeared.

"Micah, what's your location?" Shawn said into his mike after one of his men assisted in locking Jim away in a secure location just outside of the hotel.

"The west wing. Shawn, you need to see this."

Without waiting another second, Shawn gripped Cydney tighter and told his security officer to watch Jim. When he arrived outside the west wing, Shawn spotted Micah crouched down near a group of bushes. Micah turned at the sound of fallen leaves crunching under their feet.

"Take a look at this," Micah said, pointing in the distance as he handed Shawn his binoculars. "See any familiar faces?"

Shawn took the binoculars from Micah to observe the situation. About two hundred yards away stood a group of men barely visible by the lights in the parking lot. "Who are they?" Shawn asked Micah as he continued to view the men.

Micah glanced over at Cydney and then back at Shawn. "Check them out one by one," he suggested discreetly.

Shawn pushed a couple bush branches out of his way to clear his line of vision as he took a look at each of the men individually. "No, come on," Shawn said as realization hit him as to who the men were. In the parking lot in what appeared to be a business deal stood a couple of the Midwest's most influential businessmen, including men he'd seen on several occasions in the Detroit and Chicago P.D. offices.

"This is worse than I thought," Shawn said, for Micah's ears only. He peeked over at Cydney, who was now sitting on the grass with her head on her knees, no doubt still trying to comprehend what had *almost* happened to her. As if she'd heard him, she lifted her head and looked directly at Shawn, her big mahogany eyes full of questions that Shawn wasn't sure he could answer right now.

"Even worse," Micah said quietly to Shawn so that Cydney couldn't hear. "The hotel manager sensed something was wrong and called Indianapolis P.D. before I could stop her. She thought she was helping. Don't you find it odd that these men would feel comfortable enough to do business right in the open when you can hear the sirens in the distance headed this way?" Micah asked quietly so that Cydney couldn't hear.

"I guess there's no reason to leave when you have partners on the inside," Shawn said, passing the binoculars back to Micah and removing his phone to send Agent Wolfe a text message with a code they used in case one of them needed to discuss an urgent matter.

Send For
2 FREE BOOKS
Today!

I accept your offer!

Please send me two
free novels and two mystery
gifts (gifts worth about $10).
I understand that these books
are completely free—even
the shipping and handling will
be paid—and I am under no
obligation to purchase anything,
ever, as explained on the back
of this card.

168/368 XDL F429

Please Print

FIRST NAME

LAST NAME

ADDRESS

APT.#   CITY

STATE/PROV.   ZIP/POSTAL CODE

Visit us online at
www.ReaderService.com

Send For
2 FREE BOOKS
Today!

I accept your offer!

Please send me two
free novels and two mystery
gifts (gifts worth about $10).
I understand that these books
are completely free—even
the shipping and handling will
be paid—and I am under no
obligation to purchase anything,
ever, as explained on the back
of this card.

168/368 XDL F429

Please Print

FIRST NAME

LAST NAME

ADDRESS

APT.#   CITY

STATE/PROV.   ZIP/POSTAL CODE

Visit us online at
www.ReaderService.com

K-1/14-GF-13

◀ Detach card and mail today. No stamp needed. ◀ © 2013 HARLEQUIN ENTERPRISES LIMITED. ® and ™ are trademarks owned and used by the trademark owner and/or its licensee. Printed in the U.S.A.

As he was typing the message, he noticed he was receiving a call from Agent Wolfe.

"Miles," Shawn said as he answered the phone, purposely leaving out the word *agent* before he stated his name.

"Agent Miles, this is Agent Wolfe. Something has just come to my attention that may affect your case."

"I was just about to message you about another matter," Shawn said, firmly knowing Agent Wolfe would understand exactly what type of message he was referring to.

"I definitely need to hear what is going on there, but unfortunately I was going to call you, anyway, once I received notification from our inside drug source in Detroit. It appears that a few new pictures are circulating of people who are assumed to be a new threat to their operation. I'll give you fair warning that your picture surfaced as one of them and so did one of Paul Jensen."

"What? That's impossible," Shawn said lowly into the phone as he took a few steps away from Cydney and Micah. "With me being CISO for the Peter Vallant Company, I understand why I'm a threat, but Jensen is one of our secondary suspects." It wasn't his first time being targeted and probably wouldn't be his last.

"Jensen should still be watched closely," Agent Wolfe replied. "We need to keep all our options open in case this is a setup. In the meantime, I need you to be extremely alert. We take threats against an FBI agent very seriously, although I'm sure I don't need to remind you of that. However, my source did confirm that they don't know you're FBI, so we still have that working in our favor. Jensen will need to be watched 24/7 and you will need to put one other person under immediate surveillance."

"Right away, sir," Shawn said in reply to Agent Wolfe's request. "Who is he?"

"It's not a he," Agent Wolfe said with a little more concern this time. "It's Cydney Rayne. She's the third person being targeted."

Shawn's back stiffened at the sound of her name as he pinched the middle of his forehead in an attempt to stop the headache that was rising. He hadn't had this particular feeling of apprehension in three years, and suddenly past situations flooded the forefront of his mind as thoughts of something terrible happening to Cydney swarmed in his head.

"Miles, are you there?" Agent Wolfe asked. Just to be sure that he'd heard the correct name, he asked Agent Wolfe to repeat the third person being targeted once more. Hearing Cydney's name again did nothing to ease his worry. Shawn confirmed that both Paul and Cydney would have around-the-clock watch and then he updated Agent Wolfe on the current course of events. Shawn agreed to set up a conference call with Agent Wolfe, Mr. Vallant and himself in a few hours so they could update Mr. Vallant on the case and decide if they needed to postpone the rest of the appreciation events. "Keep me in the loop," Agent Wolfe said. "I have a feeling since someone has connections with the Indianapolis P.D., they won't make a big deal about the possible kidnapping. They wouldn't want to bring too much attention to themselves, but they will be looking for Jim soon, so I may have to send reinforcements."

Shawn agreed with Agent Wolfe's assessment and as he was hanging up the call, Indianapolis P.D. began to arrive at the hotel. Shawn walked over to Micah and told him they needed to get the P.D. in and out as quickly as possible. They wanted to follow protocol so that no one suspected Shawn was FBI, but they needed to maintain a low profile, as well. And Shawn needed Cydney to be on board in order to successfully do that. He walked over to Cydney, who was still sitting on the grass, and squatted down beside her.

"Cydney, I know you're scared, but you're in my care now, so you're safe." He lifted her hands in between his in an attempt to bring her comfort. Her eyes that had been staring out into the distance turned to meet his gaze. They were still watery, but she seemed to be more at ease.

"I need you to trust me," Shawn continued as he helped her rise from the grass to stand up. "In a short while, the P.D. will probably need to talk to you about what happened." He began rubbing his hands up and down her arms. "I need you to tell them that you had stepped out to get some fresh air and were grabbed. But someone heard you scream and came to your rescue."

Cydney squinted her eyes in confusion as she observed his face. "Why do I have to lie?"

Shawn chose his next words carefully. "I need you to fabricate the story, not lie."

"It's the same thing," Cydney retorted in frustration.

"Cydney," Shawn said a little softer this time. "As CISO, I need to do my job, and there is something going on here that we haven't figured out yet. My team and I want to make sure that everyone is safe."

"Isn't that why we have the police? How would you and your team do a better job than the actual police?"

"Because my team is aware of more than the police

at this time. Something isn't adding up and to be on the safe side, we need to talk to some of our connections in Chicago before information is spilled into the hands of the Indianapolis P.D."

Shawn could tell she wasn't buying his story, but he didn't need her to believe him. He just needed her to follow directions.

"Cydney, please trust me on this one. You know from the short investigation you did on Jim Pearson that something is going on way beyond the everyday crime. Don't you want to get to the bottom of this?"

He knew he had her on his side when her face softened in understanding. "Okay," she said with an easy sigh. "I trust you."

"Thank you," he said then he gave Micah a positive head nod and encompassed Cydney in a hug.

Chapter 11

Shawn sent Micah to the secure location where they were holding Jim before requesting that one of his other security guards keep watch of the situation. *Hmm... P.D. only sent two cars,* Shawn noticed in suspicion and surprise. He darted behind the side of the hotel when a couple of the businessmen he'd been watching went to the police to inquire about what was going on, stating they were contributors of the Peter Vallant Company. Although they really could be contributors, Shawn didn't believe that the cultural fair was their main reason for being in Indianapolis. In case they had connections on the inside and had seen a photo of him being passed around, Shawn couldn't risk being seen.

Once he had a secluded hiding place on the side of the building where he could still hear everyone speaking, Shawn looked over at Cydney, who was talking with a police officer. It was evident that she was still shaken up, but she was handling the situation like a pro. He overheard her sticking with the fabricated story of needing fresh air and being taken by a masked man before screaming and being rescued by someone who she didn't know.

Shawn's attention was taken away from Cydney when he noticed one of the police officers a few feet away from her. The way he was watching her made Shawn uneasy.

"Take a look at the officer on your left," Shawn said into his mike to his security guard that wasn't standing too far from Cydney. His guard turned his head slowly as if surveying his surroundings before motioning with a subtle nod that something was definitely suspicious.

The police officer looked at one of the businessmen and nodded his head in Cydney's direction. The gesture was so quick that one might not have noticed the elusive way the officer acknowledged the businessman. But Shawn was trained to notice the slightest of movements and his quick eyes followed the way the men observed one another before they both settled their eyes on Cydney.

Moments later, she had wrapped up her conversation with the police officer and had turned to walk back into the hotel. "Stay with her at all times," Shawn said to his guard as he continued to observe the men outside. Once Cydney was inside the hotel, the officer who had jotted down the details of her story walked over to the other officer and was joined by one of the businessmen. They looked from the hotel entrance and back to each other, no doubt trying to develop a plan of action.

"Shawn, Cydney is refusing to follow me and insists she be allowed to go to her hotel room to change. I'll stand guard outside," Shawn heard in his earpiece.

"Absolutely not," Shawn stated into his mike. "She

needs to be taken to our office. She's too accessible in her hotel room."

Just then, the officers got back into their police cars, and two of the businessmen walked back into the lobby. *Man, I know that guy,* Shawn thought as he observed one of the businessmen. He'd seen him on a billboard or something, but he couldn't quite place his name.

"They're coming in," he said on his mike to his security guard. "Don't take the elevator to Cydney's room, take the stairs to our location. Do you copy?"

"Shawn," Micah's voice said into his earpiece. "The light isn't flashing that indicates his mike and earpiece are on. You need to go check it out. Last place I had him was outside Cydney's room." Seconds later, Micah's voice filled the mike again. "I have a visual. Our security guard is fighting another man on the floor. The other guy is taking Cydney to the stairwell. The rest of us are on our way for backup."

Reacting as quickly as possible, Shawn entered the hotel through a side door and entered the stairwell, taking two steps at a time. When he was almost near her floor, the stairwell door above him flew open and he could hear Cydney's distressed voice.

Shawn was two floors down from them so he quietly opened the door to the floor he was on, preparing to catch the culprit off guard. Once Cydney and the man passed the door Shawn was stationed behind, he swiftly opened the door and entered the stairwell, knocking the man on the back of his neck with the bottom of his pistol. The man tumbled to the ground and almost took Cydney with him, but Shawn was quick to rescue her. Grabbing her hand and jumping over the unconscious man on the floor, Shawn didn't waste any time getting

Cydney out of harm's way. "I have her, but the guy is unconscious on the third floor," Shawn said when they exited the stairwell and ran right into a crowd of people. The event was coming to a close and attendees were beginning to leave the cultural fair.

"We caught the other guy, too," Micah's voice said through the earpiece. "We're on our way to get the guy you knocked out now." Shawn sidestepped through the mass of people as he tried to make his way to their secure office. Cydney wasn't fighting him, making the trek through the crowd a whole lot easier.

Suddenly, the hairs on the back of his neck stood on alert. Shawn stopped walking for a few seconds as he did a 360-degree turn around the crowd, making sure he kept Cydney safely tucked on his side. There were several men sprinkled in the crowd who no doubt had him and Cydney as their main course of interest.

"Cydney, we have to go for a little ride," Shawn said into her ear as he tugged her arm and ventured toward a side exit.

"Shawn, I'm scared," Cydney exclaimed behind him as they ran through the door. As suspected, a glance over his shoulder proved a few of the men were hot on their trail.

"I know, but we have to get out of here," Shawn said as he made his way to one of the vehicles he'd requested in case of an emergency. Shawn and Cydney darted through a parade of trees, leaving the hotel grounds with darkness working in their favor. The car was hidden in a parking lot behind several houses in a nearby neighborhood. Once they were inside the car, Shawn called Micah on his phone since his earpiece and mike were now out of range.

"Micah, we had to leave the hotel. There were several more men in the hotel lobby. I'll make some calls, but you and the men need to be alert. We can't trust the Indianapolis P.D. so I need you to make some calls to Chicago P.D."

"You got it," Micah replied. "We also found Paul Jensen in one of the utility closets near the conference rooms. He'd been beaten up pretty badly, but he'll be okay."

"Thanks. I'll make a call so he can be put under immediate witness protection." Shawn hung up, then hit number one on his speed dial, ignoring the curious look Cydney shot his way before he turned his head back to the window. The number he called went straight to voice mail so he was forced to leave a message.

"Agent Wolfe, this is Agent Miles," he said as he heard Cydney gasp before she placed her hand over her mouth and turned her head toward him. "We have a situation and we need backup immediately. I have Cydney Rayne, and the other victim needs to be placed under witness protection. My team is aware of the situation." He dared to look at her and instantly regretted it. Her eyes squinted together and her breathing grew more rapid. She was fuming. He could tell that she felt betrayed. He saw it in her looks and body language, but he didn't have time to dwell on the situation. He had to figure out where to take her until the FBI was able to get more answers. He didn't trust anyone right now and he refused to let anything happen to her. He knew seizing Cydney and escaping to a secure location out of the reach from any P.D. or drug-related gangs was against protocol, but reason had flown out the window the moment he'd noticed she'd been taken earlier that night. "Call me back ASAP."

After Shawn hung up the call, Cydney wasted no time asking the obvious question. "Agent Miles…as in an FBI agent?"

He looked from the road to Cydney, surprised that after tonight's events, she still looked as sexy as ever. He had enough experience to know that victims of any type of traumatic experience sometimes lashed out at those around them if they felt betrayed in any way. In this case, he didn't expect any different from Cydney.

"Yes, I'm an FBI agent," Shawn finally stated, watching Cydney as she put her head in her hands. When she lifted her head back up, her eyes were full of disbelief and astonishment.

An FBI agent? How in the world had she missed the fact that he was an FBI agent? "So," Cyd said with a slight drawl of her tongue. "What are you doing at the Peter Vallant Company?"

"Well, I run my own security firm," Shawn stated as he stared out into the dark road. "But I'm also working undercover for the FBI to try to solve a case that has taken three years to resolve."

"How long have you been with the FBI?" she asked quickly.

"Ten years," Shawn answered just as fast.

"How old are you?" she asked, a little surprised at herself for not asking him that earlier.

"Thirty-two."

"And you run your own business and work for the FBI?"

"Yes, my business is in the beginning stages."

"Then you must have a lot of resources to track people."

"I have resources and connections in the government or otherwise."

"You know a lot about me?"

"I know enough."

Hmm. "Do you mean you know me because you ran a background check or do you mean you know me sexually?"

"I take it that that is a rhetorical question, right?"

"No."

"Then the answer is both. I ran a background check and—" he said as he turned to look her straight in the eyes "—I definitely got to know you sexually."

Cyd's breath caught in her chest. *Don't salivate over him, girl. Get it together!*

"When will I be able to go home?"

"Hopefully in a week."

"A week! Where are you taking me?"

"Under witness protection…with me." *Aw, heck, naw!* She couldn't handle that. Asking him questions was not only taking her mind off what had *almost* happened to her, but it was also solidifying the fact that Shawn was a man she shouldn't be involved with. Not only was he missing attributes on her list, but he also had a dangerous job with severe consequences.

"What if I demand to go home?"

He gave her a sidelong glance. "I highly doubt you'd choose to be put in danger."

Only then did Cyd realize she'd been sitting as straight as an arrow in the passenger seat, afraid to relax until she understood what was going on. Their back and forth Q&A was exhausting, yet it was helping, and she tried to convince herself not to get upset at the man who'd recently saved her life not once, but twice. But she couldn't help how she felt, no matter how hard she tried. The fact that he hadn't told her his true occupation hurt, although deep down she understood why he couldn't. But the real kicker was the idea of her being forced to stay with him for a few days in who knows where. *That* really boiled her blood.

Cyd finally relaxed in her seat as the enormity of the possible circumstances that could have occurred enveloped her consciousness with brute force. She loved to live on the edge of danger, but she'd always gotten her thrills by leaping out of airplanes or diving into deep coves. Almost being kidnapped—twice—was *not* her idea of living dangerously. That was just plain dangerous. *Did I get myself into this trouble when I began my investigation of Jim Pearson?*

"Don't think it's your fault, Cydney." Shawn interjected her thoughts. "He'd targeted you long before you targeted him, but you're safe now."

"You know," Cyd said as she placed her right hand on the dashboard and leaned into him, "you really need to stop this whole mind-reading thing. It's beginning to creep me out." She gave a derisive look to match her sarcastic tone.

Instead of responding to her comment, Shawn gave her a penetrating stare that momentarily labored her breathing. Even with all the commotion that had happened earlier, his masculine scent encircled her nostrils and induced her desire. When he turned back to the road, Cyd took the opportunity to admire his profile. She noticed the worry lines in his brow, evidence that he was concerned about her. His right hand tightly gripped the steering wheel, flexing as he passed by cars as he switched lanes. Cyd's head dropped to the right as she studied his firm jawline. She had so many more questions she wanted to ask, but if she was honest with herself, she'd realize that she was afraid to learn all the answers, at least for tonight. She also realized that she didn't really know much about the real Shawn Miles, the man behind the devastatingly good looks and charming personality. Of all times to be mesmerized by a man, now was definitely not the best time. She thought he was mysterious before, but the man she observed now was far more mysterious than she'd imagined.

"Where are you taking me?" she asked as she leaned back to an upright forward position in her seat. He didn't answer right away and when he did, he kept his eyes glued on the road.

"I'm taking you someplace away from the public until I get a handle on what's going on."

Away from the public? "Like in the woods or something?" Cyd asked with a slight rise in her voice.

Shawn laughed at her question. "Or something," was his only answer. Only then did he glance over at her again. "Why don't you take a nap and I will wake you when we get there?"

"What about my family? They'll want to know what's going on."

"I'll call your brother-in-law Daman and he can inform your family. I want to check on a few things before you contact them directly."

"What about the rest of the events for the Peter Vallant Company?"

Shawn sighed before he responded. "Cydney, a lot has happened to you today and I need you to trust me.

I promise we will talk more once we get settled in our location."

She took one last glance at him before she rotated to look out of the window. She felt safe with Shawn, and that was really important, but she wasn't sure she liked the idea of being placed under witness protection…with him as her protector. It wasn't because she thought he couldn't protect her from the people after her. He'd already proved he could. The reason she didn't like the idea was because he was now her sole protector, and not being intimate with him was going to be an impossible task. Her mystery lover had reentered her life only to save her from evils she hadn't known were lurking. And now, headed to an unknown location, Shawn had managed to land right where she hadn't known she craved him most—her heart.

Chapter 12

"We're here," Cydney heard Shawn say as she opened her eyes and stretched her back. She'd slept for much longer than she'd anticipated, but at least she felt more relaxed than she had earlier. She yawned as she looked over at Shawn, who was exiting the car. A quick glance at her surroundings made her breath catch in her throat. It was breaking dawn outside and the autumn trees were blowing in the wind. The brilliant colors of nature and soft hum of a nearby lake was breathtaking and Cyd could have appreciated the ambiance even more if they had been standing outside a hotel rather than a cabin. A camper was one thing Cydney Rayne was not. It was not that she detested camping; she just didn't enjoy the idea of roughing it in the wilderness. There was something about the dark of the night and uncertainty of what animals prowled around that had always been her reasoning for declining any invitation to go camping. *But you've definitely never camped with a man like Shawn Miles,* the voice inside her head reminded her.

"Um, where are we?" she asked Shawn as she joined him outside the car. Instead of responding to her, he smiled and made his way to the front porch of the cabin. Cyd followed Shawn through the dirt, her bare feet growing even filthier than before. She wanted to curse Jim for numerous reasons, one, probably the silliest reason, was that he'd made her discard her shoes before they climbed down the ladder at the hotel. Shawn took the stairs two at a time and Cyd was quick on his heels, swatting at a few flies on her way to the front door.

Opening the cabin door, Shawn stepped back to let her enter. "Welcome to my cabin in Gatlinburg, Tennessee."

"Tennessee!" she exclaimed as she walked through the door, not believing that they had crossed several state lines in the middle of the night. Cyd had stopped in Tennessee briefly years ago on her way to visit some relatives, but she hadn't been able to visit much of the area. "You own this cabin?"

"Yes, I do," Shawn said as he closed the door and began opening the blinds. "This is by far one of my most favorite homes."

"One of your favorite homes?" she asked him questionably.

"Yes, I own several homes including that beach home in Anguilla. But this cabin is one of the most rural, yet relaxing, places I own."

Who is this guy? CISO turned FBI agent turned multihome owner. Seriously? "Well, your cabin is very nice."

"Thanks," he replied as he continued to open the blinds. "There are two levels, four bedrooms and two bathrooms, a fully equipped kitchen and a Jacuzzi on the back patio that I will make sure is ready for you in case you need to relax."

She followed Shawn as he took her on a tour of the cabin. Cyd admired the rustic interior with fur rugs, solid wooden chairs, enormous ten-person dining table and large-mantel fireplace. The cabin was truly gorgeous, decorated with warm colors and a comfortable setting that felt very homey. Cyd instantly felt at ease even though they were still in the middle of the wilderness. It helped that there were also large flat-screen televisions in most of the bedrooms and living room.

"When will I be able to go shopping for clothes?" Cyd asked when she realized she hadn't been able to grab anything out of her hotel room.

"My team will ship all your belongings back to Chicago. In the meantime, I called my neighbors and had them stock the shelves and the closet in your room. You'll find clothes, socks, shoes and undergarments in there."

"Is that safe? To tell your neighbors I'm here?" Cyd asked, knowing they were supposed to be in hiding.

"Definitely," Shawn replied. "I trust this couple with my life."

Just as Shawn was finishing his statement, they arrived to the room on the second floor where she would be staying. Cyd was suddenly overcome with an uneasy feeling that she couldn't shake. She didn't like the idea of other people packing up her private belongings, including her undergarments and grandmother's diaries that she treasured. The only thing she'd managed to grab before she was snatched from her room was her purse that contained a little makeup, one of the diaries and other odds and ends that she knew wouldn't do her any good now. She didn't even have her iPhone since she'd dropped it during the attack.

"I'll let you get settled," Shawn said after he'd shown her where everything was in her room. Once Shawn left, Cyd opened a couple drawers and observed the different sizes and styles that had been gathered for her. Next, she went to the closet and ran her fingers over the dresses and jeans that were hanging there. Unlike the spicy pine smell of the cabin, her room smelled of fresh lavender. Usually the smell of lavender was very calming to Cyd, but today it was a reminder that she was far from home and away from the comfort of her loved ones. She'd been through a whirlwind the past twenty-four hours and she hadn't thought she needed much comfort…until now.

Cyd plopped on the bed and dropped her head into her hands, overwhelmed by the new emotions that overtook her. She felt like her nerves had been playing a game of Ping-Pong ever since the first attack, and even though she was safe now, she still felt on edge. *Please don't cry, please don't cry,* she chanted over and over to herself. She was a strong woman who could overcome anything and she refused to let Jim and whoever else was after her get the best of her. But even as she chanted the words, she could feel the tears in the back of her eyes demanding to be released. Her adolescent ways of playing detective were long gone. Not in her wildest dreams did she imagine that one day she'd be involved in an actual case and have to be placed under witness protection.

Deciding she couldn't be in her room any longer, she made her way downstairs to the only bedroom on the lower level, the one that Shawn said he would be occupying. Instead of the bedroom, she found him on the back porch checking on the Jacuzzi. He stopped suddenly and Cyd assumed he'd noticed she was watching him through the glass door. He didn't look up at her; instead, he looked at his wet shirt as he discarded it and continued cleaning the Jacuzzi. Her eyes had a mind of their own as they took in the complete view of his naked chest. It had to be forty degrees outside, but Shawn didn't seem fazed by the weather. "Hot-blooded male," she said to herself as she continued to watch him.

After he'd checked and cleaned the Jacuzzi, he swept the fallen leaves off the porch. Watching him clean the porch with the beautiful mountains in the distance was a picturesque scene Cyd wished she could keep with her forever. *There should seriously be a rule against a man looking that handsome.* His rugged look gave him the appearance of a mountain man, further proving that she hadn't really known the man behind the city swagger and captivating wordplay. Her center grew wetter the more she stood and watched him in his element. *Oh, no, please don't chop the wood,* she thought as she watched him pick up an ax and walk over toward the tree stumps on the ground near the porch. She could barely keep her legs closed now, so watching him chop wood without a shirt would no doubt soak her panties even more. As suspected, he went about chopping several pieces of wood, her pink essence throbbing with each chop of the ax. *Lord, have mercy.* Why did he make everything look so damn sexy!

When he looked as if he was coming back into the cabin, Cyd made a beeline dash to his room to wait for him. She didn't know why she didn't just wait for him in the living room where she'd been watching him outside. All she knew is that her first thought was to catch him in his room.

This is insane, she thought to herself when she quietly sat on his bed in the most erotic pose she could think of at the moment. She had almost convinced herself to leave his room and meet him in the living room when his six-foot-three frame engulfed the bedroom doorway.

"Where are you going?" he asked her in a husky voice as he leaned one forearm against the entryway. This man had the ability to make her feel like a nervous schoolgirl, adding another emotion to her already growing list of her current feelings since the incident.

"Um, I figured I would go take a shower," Cyd lied as she fully rose from the bed and tried to make it past him.

"I saw you watching me," he said as his arm enfolded her waist and gently tugged her to his damp cinnamon chest, halting her quest to get out of the bedroom. Cyd took several breaths before she got up enough nerve to look him fully in his eyes. And when she did, all the apprehension she felt was replaced by fiery need and potent attraction. His sea-blue eyes ventured to her lips only to return with a clear agenda. "You're sexy as hell," he said to her as his eyes darted from her lips to her dress.

"I can't look sexy after everything I've been through," Cyd replied shyly. She couldn't think straight when he looked at her with such inhibition. It was rare that she'd gotten to actually see him look at her quite like that. His lips curled up in the sexiest half smile she'd seen on him yet.

"I disagree," he said, right before he leaned in a little closer to her mouth. Once he was mere centimeters away, Cyd noticed the slight look of concern in his face.

"Are you okay?" he asked in the sweetest voice. Instead of responding, she nodded her head to indicate that she was.

"Are you sure?" he asked her again, not convinced.

"At first I wasn't," Cyd admitted. "That's why I sought you out."

"And now?" Shawn said as he placed his hand gently on the back of her neck while the other remained around her waist.

"Now I'm more than okay," Cyd replied, leaving his hypnotic eyes and landing her gaze on his juicy lips. Shawn then pulled her head closer to his, their mouths fusing together in a perfect union. A moan escaped Cyd's mouth when Shawn's tongue slid through her lips evidently on a mission to bring her to her knees in desire. *Mission accomplished,* she thought as she felt herself being lifted in the air and placed gently on the bed. He slid between her legs with grace and style as his hands pushed her dress to her waist. His lips never left hers as his tongue dipped in and out of her mouth, allowing more moans to escape. He left her mouth and began placing hard kisses on her neck. His lethal tongue was no doubt leaving imprints on every part of her body that he touched. When his mouth found hers again, his kisses grew slower. Shawn stopped kissing her and lifted himself onto his hands as he gazed down at her face. When he didn't say anything but continued to look at her, she noticed that the mask that was usually blocking his true desires was left uncovered for her to observe. She felt like there were still many secrets left untold, but what gave her hope was the fact that his look proved he wanted her to know some of those secrets.

She lifted one hand to his cheek as she searched for more reasoning and answers. The passion still lingered in the depths of his eyes, but vulnerability and intense desire were also present in his look. Apparently, deciding he'd shown her enough, he rose from the bed and helped her get up, as well.

"How about we both take showers and then we'll make something to eat?" Shawn asked.

Cyd smoothed out her dress as she tried to organize her thoughts. "Sounds like a plan," she said and gave him one quick peck on the lips before escaping upstairs to her room to shower. Once she was on the other side of the door, she lay on the bed and looked up into the ceiling. *Cydney Rayne, you've really done it this time.* Although Shawn had said none of this was her fault, she suspected he was trying to ease her worry. She'd always been told that her antics would get her into trouble one day, and finally she understood just how much trouble, reflecting again on the situation she could have avoided. Now she was stuck in Gatlinburg, Tennessee, supposedly in witness protection, and all she could think about was sexing the hell out of Agent Shawn Miles. *Way to have your priorities straight, Cyd,* she said to herself sarcastically as she got up to take a much-needed shower. *Maybe all I need is some me time.* She actually hadn't relaxed in weeks and although she wasn't much of a reader, she'd noticed the bookshelf was full of great novels. "Yup, a good book should do the trick." And if it didn't, it would at least prolong the inevitable.

Chapter 13

"Come on," Shawn said to himself as he adjusted his pants for the third time this morning. He'd had a hard-on ever since he'd kissed Cydney yesterday and it still hadn't gone down. She'd politely excused herself from lunch and dinner, leaving him horny and irritated. He left her food on the outside of the door and each time, he returned to find an empty tray.

Shawn figured she was avoiding him, for what reason, he had no idea.

"Cydney, are you ready?" he yelled up the stairs. His neighbors had invited them over for brunch and Shawn was going to use the time after brunch to pick up some necessities and call Agent Wolfe. He knew his neighbors would keep Cydney busy while he handled his business and went into town to get some supplies.

Mama Jessie and Papa Willie were more than his neighbors, they were his godparents and the couple who had raised him. Mama Jessie was best friends with his mom, and Shawn would forever be grateful for the love and support he'd gotten from them.

"Here I am," she said as she made her way down the

stairs. She had on a pair of blue-jean capris and a navy blue blouse that would look modest on most women, but on Cydney, it looked sensual. "I may be a little cold, but it was hard to find pants that fit the way I needed them to," she continued to say.

"You look great," he said when she reached the bottom of the stairs, his eyes glued to the part of her legs that were showing beneath the capris.

"You look nice, too," she said with a slight gleam in her eyes.

"Finally I'm getting you out that room."

Cyd raised an eyebrow at his statement. "It's only been a few hours," she said, crossing her arms over her chest. "Besides, I'm reading a great book." Book or no book, she was definitely avoiding him. But if she wasn't ready to admit it, he wasn't going to force her. Sooner or later, she'd have no choice but to come to terms with her feelings for him.

Slow down, Miles, he warned himself. The last thing they both needed was to get too deeply involved before the case was solved. Feelings clouded judgment and Shawn was already in too deep with Cydney.

"I called Daman last night," Shawn said as he and Cydney made their way to the front door. "My neighbors live a couple miles away, so you can call your sister when we get to the car. She's expecting your call."

"Thank goodness," Cydney said as she jumped up and down with glee. "I need to talk to her so badly."

As crazy as it seemed, Shawn felt a tinge of jealousy that he wasn't the reason behind her happiness. They got into the car and Cydney wasted no time hurrying Shawn to hand over his cell phone. Imani answered on the third ring.

"This is Imani Rayne-Barker."

"Sis, it's me, Cyd."

"Oh, my God, Cyd, are you okay? Daman told me he spoke with Shawn. I've been worried sick."

"I'm fine. It's been an insane couple days, but I'm finally safe…thanks to Shawn," Cyd said as she momentarily glanced at him.

"Honestly, I would have probably gotten the girls and driven to Indianapolis myself had it not been for Shawn."

"I know," Cydney said with a sigh. "I can't believe the mess I've gotten myself into."

"Daman wouldn't tell me details, but I highly doubt any of this is your fault," Imani replied. When Shawn had told Daman some of the story, he'd left it up to him as to what he told his wife.

"Thanks, sis. Did you tell Mom and Dad I'm okay?"

"Yes, I told them that you'd fallen for Shawn and the two of you took an impromptu trip out of the country and you left your phone." Shawn choked back a laugh when all the color drained from Cydney's face. He was trying not to eavesdrop on their conversation, but it was hard considering his phone was connected to the car's speaker.

"What!? Imani, why would you tell them that?"

"So they wouldn't worry, why else! They met Shawn at the wedding and Shawn gave Daman permission to tell them he's in the FBI. They agreed to keep it secret and Mom was thrilled that you'd finally met a man." That time, Shawn couldn't hold back and let out a hearty laugh.

"But Shawn and I aren't a couple! What happens when I have to tell Mom and Dad the truth?"

"Well, little sis, my gut is telling me that you and Shawn are way past friends. Are you telling me y'all haven't had sex again since my wedding?"

"Imani, he can hear you! You're on speakerphone."

Imani laughed on the other end of the call. "Duh, I know that. Why do you think I brought it up?"

"Okay," Cyd said, clearly even more embarrassed than before. "On that note, I think I'll hang up now."

"Don't hang up on my account," Shawn interjected. "Hey, Imani," he said, greeting Cydney's sister.

"Hi, Shawn," Imani eagerly replied. "Thanks for taking care of my sister."

"It's been my absolute *pleasure*," he said, purposely insinuating that he was doing more than just protecting her. He was rewarded by a hard punch on the shoulder by Cydney.

"Cyd," Imani said. "Before I go, Lex, Mya and I have a message for you."

"Oh, really," Cyd said as she looked over at Shawn again with a look of innocence.

She wouldn't be looking at me like that if she knew how badly it made me want her, he thought.

"And what might that be?" Cyd continued.

"Daman mentioned that you'd be somewhere for a week, so if you can go grocery shopping, make sure you buy a few cans of pineapples to stock in the cabinet. Fresh pineapples are better, but I'm not sure where you are and what you have access to."

"Why would I need a bunch of pineapples?" Cyd asked in confusion. Shawn knew exactly what Imani was talking about. Pineapples were his favorite fruit and he'd read more than a few articles about its benefits.

"Pineapples are known to make the female juices

taste better," Shawn responded to her question. "The more you eat, the better you taste." He was well aware of the double meaning in his statement and his eyes landed on hers as she looked at him with awe.

"Seriously," Cyd replied in a soft, yet disbelieving, voice. "How do you know that?"

"I happen to love pineapples," Shawn answered matter-of-factly. He purposely licked his lips as he overly enunciated the last words of his next statement. "I even heard that using the fruit while making love makes for a very delicious kind of sex." His eyes darted between the road and Cydney, mesmerized by the desire building in her eyes.

"Okay," Imani said, interrupting the silence and sexual tension in the car. "Now I feel like I'm violating a special moment between you two, so I'll let you both go. Cyd, I love you! Shawn, make sure you let my sister call and check in!"

"I love you, too," Cydney said, her eyes still glued to Shawn.

"Will do," Shawn replied before disconnecting the call and turning toward Cydney again. The road demanded that he focus, so he had no choice but to retreat from her gaze. He picked up his water bottle to take a sip, grateful that he'd chosen to bring the cool liquid with him on the short trip to his neighbors' home. His body needed a dose of coolness to bring back down his suddenly hot temperature.

"I wonder what I taste like…." Cydney stated in a come-hither kind of voice that caused him to almost spit out the water in his mouth. "Guess I need to invest in some pineapples."

Once again, his eyes darted between her and the

road, the road losing the concentration battle. "From what I remember, you already taste sweet," he said, barely finding his voice after her surprise statement.

"But your tongue hasn't really dived into me yet," Cydney replied as she smacked her lips to get her point across. *Why the heck was she saying this stuff now and not when they were back at the cabin?*

"Cydney," he said in a ragged voice when he reached his neighbors' house and parked the car in their dirt driveway. "You decide to flirt now…after you ignored me most of yesterday?"

Instead of answering his question, she tilted her head to the side and gave him her million-dollar smile. He was sure that smile had brought many men to their knees in surrender, so he might as well just give up now and add his name to her list of captives.

"If this is payback for me being hot and cold with you during the appreciation tour, then I apologize. I was just trying to do my job."

She didn't say anything and her smile turned to an expression of temptation, slowly drawing him in. She deliberately stuck out her tongue and then bit her bottom lip as she placed her hand lightly on his thigh. *Don't do that.* He needed her *not* to touch him right now. They had a brunch to attend and being *excited* at brunch with neighbors he hadn't seen in a few months was a *very* bad idea. Luckily, she removed her hand after a couple strokes up and down his thigh.

Shawn had an acute ability to read between the lines, but he wasn't seeing any lines between him and Cydney…. Only an open field to play a passionate game of touch football. She had to know what she was doing to him, but she made the act of seduction look effortless.

She blew out a deep, long sigh before he heard the word *pineapples* slip through her lips. She leaned in closer to his ear and flicked the lobe with her tongue before opening the passenger door and hopping out of the car. By the time Shawn had gotten out of the car, Cydney was already on his neighbors' front porch, waiting for him to join her.

Her sister should have never mentioned pineapples. Now she had ammo to use against him, and there was no doubt in his mind that she would use this knowledge to her advantage. Hell, she'd already started using the information against him. When he got out of the car, he looked toward the sky and held out his hands in surrender.

By the time he arrived at the stairs, Willie and Jessie Johnson had already answered the door. "Shawn," Mama Jessie yelled as she ran up to him to give him a hug. "Hey MJ," Shawn said as he returned her embrace. When he was a child, unlike most three-year-olds, Shawn knew that Willie and Jessie Johnson weren't his parents. Even at a young age he'd had a keen sense of awareness. So instead of calling them Mom and Dad, Shawn referred to them as Mama Jessie and Papa Willie. "Cydney Rayne, this is Mama Jessie and Papa Willie, or MJ and PW as I affectionately call them."

"Nice to meet you both," she said as she gave each of them a hug.

"Oh, she's a beauty," Mama Jessie said as she took Cydney's hands and led her into their house.

Papa Willie slapped him on his back as they followed the women into the house. "You did good."

"Thanks, PW," Shawn replied. "But we're just friends." Cydney overheard his reply and tucked some fallen hair behind her ear before turning to give him a quick smile. *She looked sexy.*

"Shawn," Papa Willie said when they'd fully entered the home. Only then did Shawn notice he was still fixated on Cydney.

"Yes," Shawn said at Papa Willie's successful attempt to get his attention. Papa Willie looked from Shawn to Cydney once more before giving Shawn a slight nod of disbelief.

"Whatever you say, son," Papa Willie said before closing the door and leading Shawn to the dining room.

After brunch and a quick run to a nearby hardware store, Shawn returned to the Johnsons' home and went straight to the den to call Agent Wolfe, who wasted no time informing him that Jim hadn't budged and wasn't talking.

"The FBI has ways of making criminals talk, and Jim doesn't strike me as the type who can withstand any rough handling."

"My sentiments exactly," Agent Wolfe agreed. "As far as the other men, we're trying not to bring the media into this. One of the men who was trying to kidnap Ms. Rayne was Bob Noland, CEO of one of the largest fast-food chains in Illinois."

"I knew he looked familiar," Shawn interjected.

"Our assumption is that they hadn't expected to get their hands dirty and tried to take matters into their own hands when they noticed Cydney had escaped," Agent Wolfe continued. "He called his lawyer and some people in the media are beginning to get suspicious since we postponed the rest of the Peter Vallant Company appreciation tour, so we may only be able to keep this under wraps for a few more days. One thing's for sure—you need to keep Ms. Rayne safe until we find out more. Is your cabin stocked with supplies just in case?"

Agent Wolfe wasn't talking about normal supplies, but rather equipment that would help them in case they were attacked or felt threatened. The FBI had trained him well so he was ready for any situation. "Yes, I'm prepared."

"Good, I'll keep you updated. Oh, and, Shawn," Agent Wolfe continued, "other agents were questioning why you didn't bring Ms. Rayne to an FBI secure location so she could be placed in witness protection. I vouched for you, but you'd better not disappoint me."

"I assure you, sir, she will be safe here."

Agent Wolfe was the only one in the agency who knew where they were and Shawn wanted to keep it that way.

"I'm confident that you will, but I'm not stupid. You're an excellent agent and you're always on high alert. Don't let your relationship with this woman cloud your judgment."

Shawn knew that Agent Wolfe would eventually bring up the obvious. Though he hadn't really known he was going to take Cydney to the cabin until she'd fallen asleep and he felt himself turn the car in the opposite direction.

Shawn ended his call with Agent Wolfe and walked into the living room just as Mama Jessie was taking out old photo albums that contained photos of Shawn and the rest of his family. Shawn knew Cydney would have questions for him once she noticed he was in the photo albums a lot.

"Did you use to spend every summer here?" Cydney asked as she studied each page.

"Yes, something like that," Shawn replied as he adjusted himself on the sofa. Cydney flipped through a few more pages, glancing at him in between pages.

Shawn ignored the look that Papa Willie and Mama Jessie gave him as Cyd went through pictures of him with their two sons. They could obviously tell he hadn't told her his situation based on the way she was reviewing the pictures. But he didn't see any reason to tell her just yet. *I'll just tell her when we get back to the cabin,* he thought as he started a conversation with Papa Willie to get the attention off him.

"Aw, this baby is so adorable," Cydney gleefully exclaimed. "Who is the little cutie? Is this Shawn?"

Shawn, who had been engrossed in a conversation with Papa Willie, suddenly whipped his head toward the photo album. He walked over to the album to get a closer look at the picture. *That is me....* He hadn't seen a baby picture of himself in years and he honestly didn't know how he felt about seeing the picture.

"Is that you?" Cydney asked again when no one responded.

Instead of answering her, Shawn looked from Papa Willie to Mama Jessie. "How long have you guys had this picture?"

Mama Jessie got up and began stroking his back. "Willie took this picture a year after you were born, so we've had it ever since then."

Mama Jessie walked over to her husband and leaned into him as they watched Shawn's reaction to the picture. Shawn picked up the album and ran his fingers over the picture, feeling so disconnected to the people in it. He might as well be staring at strangers…himself included.

Cydney rose from her seat and placed her hand over his arm. "I'm sorry if I said anything wrong."

Shawn looked up from the picture and over at Cydney. "It's me and my parents," he whispered, surprised and angry that he'd almost forgotten how they looked. Cydney's eyes studied his face in confusion and concern. She had no idea how monumental this moment was for him, yet she was still trying to find a way to comfort him. In that moment, his breathing quickened for two reasons. One, he hadn't seen pictures of his family in over fifteen years and two, he'd never felt comfort from anyone the way he was receiving relief from Cydney.

"They died when I was three," Shawn said, a little above a whisper this time. He left out the part about how they died and luckily Cydney didn't ask him any questions. "They were both only children so I didn't have any living relatives. Papa Willie and Mama Jessie raised me like their own son and although they were great godparents and guardians, I was a very angry teenager. I got into more fights than anyone else in my school and in a rampage one day, I ran to the woods with a suitcase of family pictures and burned everything." Shawn waited for Cydney to stare at him in disbelief or shock, but she didn't. Instead, she just listened and continued rubbing his arm.

"Papa Willie eventually found me, but it was too late—I'd burned everything that was left of them. It took a day or so, but I eventually realized what I'd done." Shawn looked back down at the picture of him and his parents again. "I'd decided that from that point on I would stop thinking 'why me' and reacting out of anger and instead I would focus on being a better person…a better man. When I turned twenty-one, I bought my first property…the cabin we are staying at."

Shawn looked at Papa Willie and Mama Jessie before turning back to Cydney. "They both really helped me mold myself into a better man."

Mama Jessie dabbed a few tears. "His mom and I were best friends, and I love Shawn like one of my own," Mama Jessie said to Cyd. "And your parents would be so proud of you," she said as she looked at Shawn.

"I agree, they would. You turned out to be a remarkable man," Papa Willie said with a smile as he held his wife.

Years ago, Shawn had chosen to join the FBI to make the world a better place and to better himself in the process. He was far from perfect, and some people from his past never failed to remind him that he used to be a bad boy without a care about anything or anyone. But that was the old Shawn. The new Shawn had spent the better part of his life striving to be the best he could be. He wasn't sure if he'd ever be the type of man that left a legacy, but he planned to succeed at everything in life. *Succeed…or die trying.*

Chapter 14

As Cyd watched Shawn stare intensely at the picture, her heart ached for him. *He never told me about his parents.* She wished she'd known before she asked who was in the picture. Although he wasn't moving away from her touch, she felt his body tense under her hand.

"I'll be back," he said suddenly as he placed the album on the coffee table and began making his way to the front door.

"Shawn," Mama Jessie said as she took the picture of Shawn and his parents out of the photo album and walked over to where he was standing. "We want you to have this." She handed him the picture, but he didn't reach out for it.

"Take it," Mama Jessie said, placing the picture in his hand. Shawn gripped the photo and enveloped Mama Jessie in his arms. Cyd gave Shawn a smile when he looked at her over Mama Jessie's shoulders. When they detached, Shawn left out the front door, obviously craving fresh air. Cyd walked over to the living room window to see if he was going anywhere. She assumed he would go for a walk or get into the car and take a ride.

Instead, he paced back and forth on the dirt driveway, looking at the ground and kicking small rocks that were barely visible. *Goodness, that must be a terrible feeling,* Cyd thought to herself. She didn't even want to think about losing her parents. *I wonder how they died?* She was afraid to ask him when he had told her that they'd passed away, but she was so curious.

"He really likes you, you know," Mama Jessie said, interrupting her thoughts.

"Honey, stop," Papa Willie said playfully to his wife. Cyd turned around when she heard movement behind her. Mama Jessie came to stand beside her at the window.

"You like him, too," Mama Jessie said a little lower so her husband couldn't hear. Cydney didn't say anything. She really had no idea how to respond to Mama Jessie's comment.

"So, Cydney, let me ask you something," Mama Jessie stated. "How does Shawn seem to you right now? Outside kicking dirt and looking overwhelmed by his past. He's grown a lot since his rebellious teenage days, but—"

"I used to be rebellious, too, so that doesn't bother me," Cydney interrupted, although she hadn't meant to.

"What I'm saying is that right now, he doesn't look like the successful and confident man he has grown to be. Going down memory lane is reverting him back to those teenage years and provoking those feelings he used to have when he believed it was him against the world."

"Part of him still feels that way," Papa Willie added, proving he could still hear them talking. "Sorry, honey, you never could whisper."

Mama Jessie gave her husband a forgiving smile before turning her attention back to Cyd. "So what do you think he needs right now?"

Cyd tilted her head to the side and observed Shawn a little more closely. Every now and then, he would look back to the house as if he was waiting for something… or someone. He looked so defeated and all Cyd wanted to do was make him feel better, like he was king of the world—her world.

She shook her head slightly to clear her mind before answering. "He looks like he needs comfort or something to get his mind off the past that is clearly haunting him right now."

"Bingo! Told you she was a smart girl," Mama Jessie said with a laugh as she turned to her husband, then back to Cyd. "So why are you still in here with us?"

Cyd looked at Mama Jessie to respond but couldn't think of anything to say. *Is she suggesting what I think she's suggesting?*

"Go ahead," Mama Jessie said while she led Cyd toward the front door, with Papa Willie right behind them. "He needs comforting, and you want to comfort him, so you're wasting time being in here with us."

When Mama Jessie opened the door, she called Shawn to the door and gave them both hugs goodbye. Cyd expected Shawn to ask why they were leaving, but he didn't say anything. He actually looked relieved, although he hadn't said anything since she'd stepped out of the house. When he started up the car, they waved goodbye and began their short journey to the cabin. During the entire two miles, Shawn didn't say anything to her. She couldn't even tell how he was feeling. *Was he mentally exhausted? Angry? Sad?*

When they reached the cabin, Shawn got out of the car, promptly took some bags out of the trunk and went over to open the passenger door for Cyd. It was dark outside now, but she noticed him study their surroundings outside before he opened the cabin door. She waited until the door was fully closed, the alarm was turned off and a couple lamps were turned on before she said anything to him.

"Shawn, are you okay?"

"I'm fine," he said as he kicked off his gym shoes and dropped the bags on the floor near the door. "Just hungry as hell."

"Okay, no problem. I can fix you something to eat," she responded, kicking off her shoes, as well. "We haven't had dinner yet. What do you want to eat?"

He walked to stand in front of the couch, but the light from the lamp didn't quite reach his face so Cyd walked over to where he was standing. The minute she reached him, he pulled her to the couch, landing her on the side of him. When the light hit his eyes, she didn't see anything reflected in them but untamed animalistic lust, and the sight made her breath catch in her throat.

"I'm not hungry for food, Cydney," he said as he gently grazed her cheek with the back of his hand. "I'm hungry for you." With that, he adjusted her perfectly on her back, his hands already unzipping her capris and sliding them down her legs.

Now would be the time to stop him, she thought to herself when her capris slipped completely off, followed by her shirt. When his hands reached the top of her panties, he gazed up at her. At first, she thought he was waiting for confirmation so that he could continue. A closer look proved he wasn't waiting for confirmation at all. From the times they'd made love, she'd realized that he liked to look into her eyes when they connected in such an intimately indescribable way. He was doing that now. Intently watching her before they connected. Before he ravished her body. She opened her mouth. To say what, she wasn't sure. It didn't matter what she'd planned on saying because the only sounds that escaped her mouth were echoes of her surrendering to the sweetest seduction.

Shawn grabbed a remote off the side table and pressed it toward the stereo. Instantly, one of Robin Thicke's latest hits began playing through the speakers. Shawn snapped her panties off within seconds and entered two fingers deep inside her core. Cyd moaned even louder as her body began moving to the rhythmic pump of his fingers. Without warning, Shawn replaced his fingers with his mouth as he slightly lifted her off the couch so that he could grip her butt in his hands and secure her to his mouth.

"Oh, my," were the only words that escaped her lips as his tongue lapped her like a melting ice cream cone. She was supposed to be making him feel better, yet he was definitely exciting her in ways he hadn't before. When his tongue circled her nub and gently sucked her essence to the beat of the music, Cyd was sure she'd squirt her juices all over if he continued.

"I'm…close…to…climaxing," she warned him, her words scarce and scattered. Instead of stopping the erotic pleasure, his strokes grew deeper and stronger. When his tongue left her nub and dived into her center, she could hear the wet noises ringing off the walls.

She climaxed—hard. She was overflowing with desire and barely comprehended that Shawn hadn't stopped after her climax. She placed her hands on his head to push him away since the feeling was too powerful and never had she come twice back-to-back. Her hands denied her request and instead of pushing him away, they held his head in place as her hips lifted to meet each plunge of his tongue into her center.

Without warning, Shawn got off the couch and kneeled down while flipping Cyd to sit upright. He threw both her legs over his shoulders and pulled her closer to his mouth. *Oh, my goodness, what is he doing to me?* The stimulating foreplay she was having with Shawn definitely beat the basic canoodling she'd experienced with past lovers. When she felt herself on the brink of another orgasm, she didn't even bother to warn him. He knew what he was doing to her and Cyd wasn't sure her body could handle a stronger onslaught of his mouth.

"Oh…my," she screamed as her body combusted into a billion pieces of passionate pleasure.

"Hmm…your taste reminds me of delicious diced pineapples laced with brown sugar," Shawn said as he lifted his head and wiped the remnants of her juices from around his mouth.

Shawn quickly went to the discarded bags at the door, opened a box of condoms and took one out. He took off his jeans and shirt and put the condom in place before making his way back to Cyd to remove her bra, the only clothing she was still wearing. Only when Shawn had effortlessly lifted her off the couch did Cyd notice a large bearskin rug sprawled out in front of the fireplace. He placed her there, gently, before he positioned himself on top of her. Although his mouth had gone to work on her center moments earlier, he eased into her nice and easy so that she could familiarize herself with the length of him again.

Shawn looked into her eyes when he began moving in and out of her with purpose and skill. What she saw embedded in the depths of them nearly took her breath away. It may seem crazy, but Cyd swore Shawn looked at her as if he never wanted to let her go. As if she were a prize that he wanted to keep forever. Cyd knew there was no way that was true, considering they'd known they weren't meant to last forever, ever since the first time they'd made love on the beach of Anguilla. But if only for tonight, she planned on pretending that he really wanted to keep her forever. She entertained the blissful idea that he could actually be her Mr. Right. That he could be that one man who she'd realize she couldn't live without.

Stroke for stroke, Shawn managed to go deeper than before, implanting himself in parts of her inner body she hadn't known existed. The curve of his manhood poked and played with her G-spot, threatening to give her another release more powerful than the past two. She wrapped her legs around his waist and lifted her hips to the movement of his.

"Cydney," he grunted with a loud and powerful rasp as they both indulged in the sinful pleasure. Shawn pumped even faster and his head dropped back toward the ceiling. Cyd couldn't understand his incoherent speech, but his sporadic actions proved he was close to his breaking point.

Cyd wanted to wait until he released himself so they could climax together. A few minutes later, he surrendered to his desire and came inside her with a force much stronger than Cyd had expected. She freed her third climax along with his, savoring the satisfying feeling that overtook her body. When the feeling subsided, Shawn lay down beside her.

"That was amazing," Shawn said as he stretched out his body.

"I agree," Cyd said, rising just enough to prop herself on the palm of her hand. She was well aware that she was still completely naked and giving him a great view of her body by leaning up, but she didn't mind. She wanted him to see her—all of her. And after everything they'd done, it seemed silly to cover herself.

The room grew quiet, each of them apparently wrapped up in their own thoughts. "Do you want me to make you something to eat now?" Cyd asked as she thought about how that question had gotten her in trouble the last time she asked.

"Sure," Shawn said as his hand began rubbing up and down her arm. "We need to eat something to keep up our strength."

"I agree," Cyd said with a slight laugh as her eyes ventured the entire length of him spread out on the bearskin rug. *He even makes breathing look sexy,* Cyd thought as she continued her admiration. *How crazy is that! Since when do I find a man sexy after sex?* She could admit to herself that she was more of a love-'em-and-leave-'em type of woman, never wanting to cuddle after sex and most times not even finding the man that tempting afterward. Her friends often teased her by saying she was more of the man in a relationship and usually, she agreed with them...until now. Shawn made her feel *all* woman, which begged the question, was there ever any man in her past who she even felt remotely connected to like Shawn? The answer was simple—never. *Gracious, the man looked sexy lounging on the rug.* If she didn't get a grip, she'd be the person initiating another round of lovemaking.

Instead, she leaned over and gave him a soft kiss on the lips. Shawn pulled her on top of him, his hands gripping both back cheeks as the kiss deepened. Her hands made their way to his hair, enjoying the soft silkiness.

"We should probably make dinner," Cyd said, breaking the kiss. Shawn gave her two more sweet pecks before he nodded his head in agreement.

Cyd stood first and helped Shawn to his feet. She was heading to the kitchen, but stopped when she felt Shawn's hand on her arm.

"Thank you," he said, pulling her into his embrace. "I needed that." She didn't need him to explain what he meant. She knew he'd needed her once she saw him pacing outside Willie and Jessie Johnson's home. To be honest, she was glad that he'd needed her. It made her feel like she was more to him than just a bed partner, and *that* was a feeling she was definitely holding on to for as long as she could.

Chapter 15

While Shawn was in his office checking emails, he could hear the click-clacking of dishes in the kitchen. Last night, Cydney had whipped up steak and mashed potatoes that were so delicious Shawn's mouth was still watering. Tonight, Cydney had insisted on washing the dishes since he'd cooked his famous lasagna for dinner. He hadn't originally planned to cook the lasagna, but when he noticed he had all the ingredients, he wanted to cook something special for Cydney after a full twenty-four hours of intense lovemaking. Never had he wanted to cook anything special for a woman before. Most women didn't even know he could cook. Mama Jessie had made sure that Shawn had all the makings to be a great husband and provider, but Shawn had never chosen to share his attributes with a woman…until he met Cydney. Since meeting her, his life felt more purposeful and all he wanted to do was make her happy. But he knew his time with her was short-lived.

Shawn had made a promise to himself years ago that he would never bring a woman into his world. He'd seen a lot of stuff in his line of work and because of some tough cases that he'd cracked, he had more than a few people who wanted to see him dead. One could argue that a lot of those men were now behind bars, but the fact still remained that criminals often had people on the outside who continued to do their dirty work while they were locked up. News about the arrests that Shawn had successfully helped make years ago was dying down, but he was still on a quest to solve the last piece of the puzzle.

He reopened an email from Malik that had been sent to him and Micah. Everyone they'd originally investigated seemed to be clear. He received the same message from the FBI. *Damn, what am I missing?* Leaning back in his office chair, he closed his eyes and crossed his hands in his lap as he did every time he was gathering all the facts in his head. *Lead Detroit drug dealer locked up three years ago? Check. Peter Vallant van used to transport drugs? Confirmed. Jim Pearson is the mole in the Peter Vallant Company? Yes. Leading businessmen involved in dirty crime. Affirmative.* His phone rang, interrupting his thoughts.

"Agent Miles," Shawn said as he got up to close the office door.

"Shawn, it's Malik. I found some more information."

"Shoot."

"It turns out that Paul Jensen is a cousin of TJ Desmond." Shawn fell back into his desk chair at the mention of TJ's name.

"Are you sure?"

"Absolutely. It took me a while to find out the information. Looks like Paul went to great lengths to conceal his identity, no doubt trying to get revenge on someone. My guess is that Jim Pearson was his target or he thought he could lead him to his target."

"That explains a lot," Shawn responded as he thought back to Paul's behavior during the appreciation tour. "Did you find out anything else?"

"Not yet, but if I do I'll give you a call."

"Thanks, Malik," Shawn said before he hung up the phone and made a call to Agent Wolfe. Agent Wolfe was happy to get the information and put in a request to question Paul Jensen right away.

Shawn thought back to Agent Wolfe's words during their last conversation. Was Agent Wolfe right? Was being around Cydney making him lose his focus? Truthfully, no one would have known about Paul since it was clear he'd paid someone off to cover his true identity. And Shawn had indeed known that something was up with him, he just hadn't placed exactly what it was. But still, Agent Wolfe's words haunted him and made him second-guess his ability to be successful at his job and fall for a woman at the same time. *Fall for a woman....* Oh, yeah, he was definitely falling hard. *What am I going to do about my feelings for her?*

His head jerked when he heard a knock on the door. "Come in," he said as he waited for Cydney to enter. She peeked her head in the door first before coming completely into the office. She was wearing a black jumper that she'd put on after a recent lovemaking session. *Is there anything this woman wears that doesn't make her look sexy?* Even in clothes that Mama Jessie had stocked for her, Cydney still looked beautiful and stylish.

"I'm finished washing the dishes and started a movie. Do you want to watch the movie with me?"

A movie with Cydney sounded great, but Shawn

had way too much on his mind to focus on a movie. "I think I'll pass," he said as he tried to give her his best genuine smile.

"Okay," she said, although she didn't leave the office. She tilted her head to the side and squinted her eyes like she always did when she was observing his behavior.

"What's wrong?" she asked, crossing her arms over her chest.

"Nothing," Shawn lied as he closed out of his email.

Cydney squinted her eyes once more. "I don't believe you," she said as she made her way to him, pushing a few papers on the desk out of her way before she sat down. Shawn leaned back in his chair and looked up at her. She looked good sitting on his desk, and immediately his mind started thinking about all the naughty things they could do in his office.

"Get your mind out of the gutter, Miles," Cydney said with a giggle. "Tell me what's wrong. I already know that something is going on, but I don't know any details. Considering I'm here with you under witness protection, I think I deserve to know what's going on."

Shawn ran his fingers down the front of his face as he contemplated what he should do. He knew he shouldn't tell her everything, but something inside him wanted to open up to her. He kept so many secrets bottled inside and only a few select individuals actually knew the real Shawn Miles. Most people only knew the persona that he portrayed to the outside world. But Cydney wasn't just anyone. She was a woman who had sneaked her way into his heart before he knew what hit him. He wasn't ready to completely come to terms with his feelings for her because he suspected that she felt the same way. Shawn had accepted years ago that he would never, ever fall for someone to inevitably put them in the lines of danger. But no matter what the future held for them, he wanted to tell her the truth.

"Do you remember when I told you that my parents died when I was three?"

"Yes, of course."

"Well, they didn't exactly die when I was three," Shawn said, taking a deep breath. "They were murdered in our Detroit home."

Cydney's hands rushed to her mouth to cover her loud gasp. "Oh, Shawn…"

"I know, it took PW and MJ years to tell me the story," Shawn said, secretly encouraging himself to continue. "My father owned a cleaners that was located right under our apartment. He never turned away customers and was a community activist in our neighborhood. A lot of people looked up to him and at the time, my father believed he could turn any criminal into a man of God. One day, a young cat by the name of Leon Roberts walked into my dad's cleaners, walked straight to the front of the line and demanded my dad take him before his other customers because he had spilled something on his favorite shirt. My dad, being the fair man he was, told him that he had to wait in line like everyone else, despite the fact that the people standing in line had allowed Leon to cut them rather than be subject to problems later. But my dad wasn't having that. Leon took his clothes and left, but not before he yelled a bunch of expletives and threatened my dad that he'd be back."

Cydney sat still on the desk, her hands now removed from her mouth and placed on the sides of the desk. Shawn adjusted himself to sit more upright in his chair before continuing.

"After that day, my dad found out that Leon Roberts was assumed to be the up-and-coming drug dealer, having recruited young men and women from all over the state of Michigan. My dad was furious and began rallying others in the community to take a stand and fight for their community. From what PW and MJ were told from people in the neighborhood back then, Leon and his growing team quickly looked at my dad as a threat. He couldn't even walk down the street without someone following him or yelling at him by claiming that he wasn't really a black man and shouldn't even be in their neighborhood."

"Why would they say that?" Cydney asked.

"Because my dad was a Creole from Louisiana with lighter skin and blue eyes and my mom was a Detroit native who used to date Leon's uncle before she met my dad and realized she deserved better."

"Oh, my goodness," Cydney said as she moved closer to Shawn. "Was Leon's uncle in the drug business?"

"Until the day he died of lung cancer," Shawn replied. "Leon's father died young so his uncle, who wasn't that much older than him at the time, was more like a brother to him and no doubt had told Leon all about the situation with him and my parents."

Shawn stopped talking as he gathered together his next thoughts, realizing just how long it had been since he told this story. "By the time I was born, my dad was still fighting for a greater cause, but after five years of fighting, my parents decided to leave Detroit after my third birthday and make a permanent home in Tennessee."

Shawn looked at Cydney's eyes that were already

filling with tears. "Maybe I should stop this story. It's pretty depressing."

"I can handle it," Cydney said as she scooted closer to him. Shawn wasn't sure he wanted to continue, but Cydney was intently waiting to hear the rest, so he kept talking.

"Word circulated in the neighborhood that they were leaving, and the night before they were scheduled to move to Tennessee, my dad's cleaners was robbed. He went down to stop the culprit and was shot and died instantly. And the robbers didn't stop there. They went upstairs to find my mom and me. We were hiding in the closet. By the time police arrived, both of my parents had been killed and for whatever reason, they'd decided to let me live. Everyone knew Leon was behind their deaths, but back then, so many people were getting killed, the police had their hands tied. No one could touch Leon and his team."

Shawn noticed Cydney shiver a little as the tears that had formed in her eyes began to fall. He stood up in front of her and began gently wiping the tears from her face.

"That's so terrible," Cydney said as she pulled Shawn into a hug. "I'm so, so sorry."

Shawn accepted her comfort and leaned his chin on the top of her head as he continued to hug her. "What happened to Leon Roberts?" Cydney asked as she looked up into his eyes.

"That's a better story," Shawn said with a slight smile. "After I got my act together, I realized that I excelled in all the qualities needed to be a successful FBI agent. One of the main reasons I joined the FBI was to help fight for families who went through what my family went through. I met my boss, Agent Wolfe, when I was in college and was quickly recruited to the FBI shortly after. I had a lot of small cases in the beginning, but then I got put on the case to bring down Leon Roberts. After years of wanting to put that man behind bars, I helped the FBI convict him, and he's currently serving life imprisonment without parole."

"That's great to hear," Cydney said with a smile.

"It is," Shawn responded. "Only we weren't able to eliminate the entire drug operation. We had a key witness who was a teenager named TJ, who for whatever reason had become one of Leon's favorite rookies. When he got caught stealing, the FBI made a promise to reduce his jail time if he helped them bring down Leon. The boy agreed and I was placed on his case to protect him. But Agent Wolfe noticed I was getting too close to the boy and took me off the case."

Cydney started rubbing her hands up and down Shawn's back when he didn't continue right away. "I saw something in him," Shawn finally stated. "I had flashes of myself when I was a teenager and instantly I wanted to help the boy. I made a promise to keep him safe and one rule that FBI agents are always supposed to follow is to *never* make promises. The day TJ was to appear in court, he was shot on his way to the courthouse and permanently paralyzed."

"Oh, no, Shawn," Cydney said again as she continued to rub his back. "I know you were devastated."

"I was," Shawn said. "The case was pushed back and we were still able to convict Leon without TJ's testimony. But TJ and his family never forgave me for not being there. I haven't seen him since that day at the hospital when he was told he would never be able to walk again."

"But it wasn't your fault. You were taken off the case."

"Yeah, but I still should have protected him."

"Shawn," Cydney said, taking his face in her hands. "You aren't Superman. You can't save everyone. You couldn't have predicted something would happen to TJ on his way to the courtroom just like your dad couldn't predict that his refusal to serve Leon before the other customers would result in years of watching his back."

Shawn looked into her eyes that were still misty with tears. "You're an amazing man with compassion and loyalty for others. What you've overcome in your life is truly admirable. Don't you know how great you are?"

My compassion? Didn't she know that her compassion was the only thing that had given him the courage to tell her the entire story? Thinking back on the past times he'd told the story, he remembered leaving out key points that he didn't leave out with Cydney. Surprisingly, telling her the entire truth gave him a very serene feeling, which completely contradicted the way he should be feeling after sharing such a devastating story.

She's got you, Miles, the voice inside him said. *She's stolen your heart and you've given her a piece of yourself that will forever be hers.*

Chapter 16

The bulge in his pants began to rise the longer he looked into her eyes. He'd already released so much pent-up emotion, yet all he wanted to do was release himself even more…preferably deep inside of her.

"Wrap your legs around my waist," he told her. She quickly obeyed and when she was secure, he lifted her from the desk and took her into his bedroom.

"Do you realize that we haven't actually had sex in the bedroom yet?" he asked her as he placed her on the bed.

"Then what are you waiting for, Agent Miles?" Cydney replied as her breasts popped free when she pushed her jumper as far down as she could while he was on top of her. He took care of the rest, discarding their clothes in the corner of the room.

"I want to get on top," she said as she scooted from underneath him. He obliged her request and lay on his back.

"You are one sexy man, Agent Miles," Cydney said in a seductive voice as she crawled in between his legs.

He waited for her to make her way up his body, but when she reached his midsection, she lingered there.

"Have I told you how badly I've been dying to taste you?"

Say what? Did she just say what I think she said? Shawn swallowed a big gulp of air. "Taste me?" he repeated to clarify if he'd heard her correctly.

"Yes," she said as she placed her hand completely around his shaft. "Taste you." She licked her lips to emphasize her point and was rewarded by his member jumping at the sound of her voice and the movement of her hand. Cydney lowered her mouth onto him, taking in his complete length, which was *not* an easy task. Some women couldn't even handle him sexually because he was larger than they expected, yet Cydney had managed to completely surround him in her mouth.

"Ooh wee," were the words that escaped his mouth as she began to move up and down. "How are you—" His speech was momentarily staggered when she began to move her mouth faster, moaning every time he reached the hilt of the back of her throat.

"I did throat massages earlier today," she stated in between licks. "I wanted to make sure I could take *all* of you."

"You did not just say that," Shawn said at the idea that sucking him into submission was something she had preordained and even practiced for.

"Oh, yes, I did," Cydney said, moving her hands up and down as she played with his tip. "You should probably buy more bananas."

"Never, and I mean never, have I met a woman like you," he said breathlessly as he gripped the sheets when she began fondling him, as well. *Dang, she says what-*

ever is on her mind. Shawn was so engrossed in the foreplay that he knew he was on the brink of a hard and long orgasm. But he didn't want to release himself that way. He wanted to feel her wrapped around him. Tight. Wet. But Cydney wasn't having that.

"Cydney, I want to come inside you," he exclaimed as he leaned up on his elbows and tried to switch positions. She looked up at him, her mouth still attached to him as she licked his shaft up and down, her eyes never leaving his.

Cheeks clenched. Jaw set. Hands in motion. Shawn had to accept the inevitable—Cydney Rayne wasn't letting him go anywhere! In all his thirty-two years he'd never come during oral sex. After living a life where nothing had been in his control, Shawn decided long ago if it were in his power to control, then he would definitely do things on his own terms. But clearly Cydney Rayne didn't know that about him. Or she knew that he liked to be in control but didn't care.

"Oh, shoot," he said aloud, dropping his head back to the bed when he felt a tingling sensation start at his feet and make its way up his legs. Cydney must have sensed it, too, because she quickened her licks, suckling him in between the strokes of her tongue. Within seconds of his statement, he released himself into her mouth as his body jerked at the intensity of his climax.

When his spasms had subsided, Cydney crawled up to him and curled herself into the nape of his neck. "That was amazing," she said as she wrapped her arms around him.

"Amazing for you?" he exclaimed. "Hell, that was incredible, remarkable and any other word you can say to imply that something was out of this world."

She laughed at his statement and tenderly kissed him on his cheek before her eyes fluttered closed. He followed suit and closed his eyes as he pulled her even closer to him. *Way to go, Miles. Way to fall for the one person you should be protecting.* He'd probably fallen for her way before he'd known she would need his protection, but that was the crux of the problem. Shawn popped open one eye to gaze down at the now-sleeping Cydney. She was everything he'd always wanted and had convinced himself he couldn't have. Now that he'd found her—the one woman he couldn't live without—there was absolutely no way he was giving her up.

Cyd was the first to wake the next morning. The rays of sunlight shining through the blinds on the window landed right on Shawn's body, accentuating the entire length of his naked masculinity. With one hand, she ran her fingers over his abs, admiring how magnificent they looked when he flexed them during their lovemaking sessions.

They had both woken in the middle of the night when Shawn's phone had rung. After his call, he'd explained the rest of the case to Cyd and told her how the Peter Vallant Company, Jim Pearson, Paul Jensen and now Bob Noland, CEO of a chain of fast-food restaurants, played a part in everything. Toward the end of the story, she'd asked him if she was in a lot of danger and he'd told her no, but not before she'd seen his hesitation. He seemed to be keeping something from her, and if she had to guess, she'd assume that someone in the drug business hadn't liked her snooping and was still after her.

Her eyes left his abs and went to his face. She was

honored that he felt close enough to her to discuss his past and in some ways, his present, as well. He'd gone through more pain in his thirty-two years than many people went through in a lifetime. Yet he'd chosen to take his pain and use it as a platform to mold himself into a better man.

Cyd eased herself out of bed, careful not to wake Shawn. Once she was out of the bedroom, she tiptoed up the stairs to her bedroom and went into her purse to find the only diary she had with her. She plopped onto the bed and positioned herself on her elbows as she skimmed the back pages, trying to find the list Gamine had written about the signs of knowing you're in love. Once she found the passage, she read each and every number on the list carefully with a newfound understanding of the meaning behind each number. She paid particular attention to the last and final number on the list. "Number twenty. He may not be perfect…but he is perfect for me," she read out loud. It was a simple line that contained a whole lot of meaning.

Closing the diary, Cyd lay on her back and stared up at the ceiling. Based on the way they'd met, Cyd would have never guessed that she would fall for Shawn Miles. She'd never thought he had any of the qualities she desired in a man to *love,* only a man to *lust.* But in actuality, he had more qualities of a man you love and lust instead of one over the other.

"Oh, goodness, I've fallen in love with him," she said to herself as she placed her hands over her face. She'd fallen for a man that she'd never seen coming and had given him a piece of her heart that she feared she'd never get back. Not that she wanted to get anything that she'd given to him back. She wanted him to keep every piece of her that he had for as long as he wanted, and *that* was a huge thing for her to admit. The fear came from the fact that she didn't think she could ever find a man more perfect for her than Shawn if they didn't end up together.

She analyzed everything that had happened since that fateful day they met in Anguilla. Shawn hadn't actually expressed any interest in building a relationship with her, which gave her an uneasy feeling in the pit of her stomach. *What do I do if he doesn't want a relationship with me?* She could tell by the way he looked at her that he had feelings for her, but she didn't dare ask him if he wanted a relationship. Although she now knew why he'd blown her off those times before, she couldn't shake the feeling of rejection that was his doing. She was hoping that he would make the first move and indicate what he wanted from her and what he was feeling. The more she thought about Shawn, the more she realized he was the type of man who probably didn't attach titles to his relationships. *But that's exactly what this feels like....*

"When did you leave the bedroom?" Shawn asked as he filled her doorway. She hadn't even heard anyone moving in the house.

"Sorry," Cyd said, sitting upright in the bed. "I didn't want to wake you."

Shawn made his way over to the bed and leaned down to give her a kiss. The sweet kiss quickly turned into a full-on make-out session that was obviously heading to something else.

"I have to take a shower," Cyd said when Shawn's kisses had moved from her lips to her neck. He stopped kissing her and flashed a wicked smile.

"Shall we shower together?" he asked, already standing and leading them both to her bathroom.

"You're insatiable," Cyd said with a laugh as she let him lead her to the bathroom.

"What can I say, baby," he said, joining her in laughter. "My loving is limitless." He pulled her into another kiss at the same time he masterfully turned on the shower. Cyd knew what he meant by the description of his sex drive, but she was hung up on the "my loving" part of his statement. *I wish you really did love me,* she thought to herself, finally, completely admitting that she was craving Shawn in every way possible.

Shawn got in the shower first, allowing Cyd a few moments to watch the water hit his body from a short distance away. When she entered the shower, Cyd squeezed some shower gel into the loofah and began rubbing the lathered suds all over Shawn's body.

"I must really like you," Shawn said with a laugh.

"Why do you say that?" Cyd asked as she continued to clean his body.

"Because I'm letting you wash my body with this girly soap."

Cyd looked at the bottle before she resumed washing him. "It's vanilla, a gender-neutral scent."

"No, it's not," Shawn said with another laugh. "Women say that so poor suckers like me won't complain when a gorgeous woman rubs the scent all over their body."

"So you think I'm gorgeous, huh?" Cyd said as she wiped his chest in a circular rotation.

"You're all right," Shawn answered.

"Not funny," Cyd exclaimed as she softly punched him in his arm.

"I'm just joking," he said as he took the loofah, squeezed on more shower gel and began rubbing it over her body.

Cyd relished in the seductive way he massaged the soap into her body. "You're absolutely gorgeous," Shawn said between strokes.

"Thank you," Cyd said placing her hand on the wall of the shower.

"Open your legs for me," Shawn requested. She did as he asked, her desire building stronger every second.

Shawn took the loofah and rubbed it between her legs, paying close attention to her throbbing bud of nerves. Her labored breathing made him increase his hand motion and push her even closer to her breaking point.

Oh, wow, she thought as she forced her eyes to hold Shawn's gaze. She'd never known how much pleasurable friction one could get from a loofah and hot water. Or maybe Shawn was just that great at understanding the inner workings of the female body.

"I'm just that good," he said, reading her thoughts once again. Cyd didn't even question it anymore and accepted the fact that this man was just connected to her and knew her better than most people she'd known for twenty-seven years. Right before she was about to come, Shawn suddenly stopped and connected their bodies with one quick thrust. Cyd looked down at their connected bodies and noticed the end of the condom peeking out between them.

"When did you put that on?"

"Like I said, I'm just that good," Shawn replied with a wink. "Lift up your left leg."

Once her leg was lifted, he grabbed her thigh to keep

her in place as he thrust in and out of her body. The combination of water hitting her clit while he rhythmically danced in her core was nearly her undoing. She watched him drop his head back and let the water hit his face. She had no idea how he was able to breathe, but watching him sex her with the water running down her body was way more erotic than she'd ever imagined.

Since arriving at the cabin, their sex and foreplay had been lengthy and satisfying. This time was definitely going to be just as satisfying, but she doubted it would be long. She'd give them two more minutes before they were ready to release the tension that was building up in their bodies.

"Oh, man, Cydney, I'm about to come," Shawn yelled, signifying that her prediction of two minutes was way too long.

"Me, too," she declared as she leaned into his thrusts by moving her waist in a circular motion while he continued to pump in and out. Her movement pushed Shawn over the edge, causing him to howl at the ceiling after his release.

Once they floated down from cloud nine, they quickly rinsed their bodies and got out of the shower. Shawn seductively dried her off before drying himself. Shawn then carried her to the bedroom, lightly placing her on the bed. He was just leaning down to kiss her when his phone rang.

"Hold that thought," he said before hopping off the bed and running down the stairs. *That was amazing,* Cyd thought in regards to her first time making love in the shower. Shawn was an expert lover, and a quick stretch of her body proved that she'd worked muscles she hadn't used in a long time. And those muscles had definitely never been worked the way Shawn worked them.

After several minutes, Cyd went downstairs to see why he hadn't returned yet. She found him in his bedroom, still on the phone. He gave her a quick smile when she walked into the room and sat on his bed.

"Yes, I will. See you soon," he said as he hung up the phone.

"Who was that?" she asked, noting that he didn't seem as happy as he'd been moments prior to the phone call.

"That was Agent Wolfe," Shawn said as he placed his phone back on his nightstand. "I guess the honeymoon is over. I need to bring you back to Chicago. We'll leave this afternoon."

Cyd noticed that he was searching her face. *Did he think I'd be excited by the news? Heck, no!* She still had no idea where their relationship stood and going back to Chicago meant going back to reality.

"So they caught everyone involved?" she asked.

"The FBI and P.D. are confident that they've caught everyone involved and the DEA is setting a plan into place to bring down the entire operation. Paul Jensen sang like a canary when he was questioned and admitted that he had been after Jim Pearson ever since he'd gained employment at the Peter Vallant Company. Paul figured Jim was key in his quest to get revenge for TJ. He also admitted to knowing who I was the week I began working for the company. Like his family, he also blamed me for allowing harm to come to TJ, but he believed there had to be a reason I was at the company three years after the case. I guess he was conflicted when we met because we got along so well and he wanted me to do whatever I needed to do to find justice. I don't think he's a bad guy, but he'll probably do some time for premeditating revenge, even though he never actually got the chance to harm anyone."

"That's sad," Cyd said, sympathizing with Paul. Shawn had a look of apprehension on his face and Cyd could feel his tension. "Are you confident they caught everyone?"

He looked at the floor before looking back at her, as if he were trying to gather his thoughts. "No," he said as he sat on the bed next to her. "But of course, I've been told that I'm paranoid at times. Until I feel comfortable with this situation, I'm not letting you out of my sight."

She saw the worry in his eyes, and although it warmed her heart, she wasn't sure if his worry was misplaced. "Shawn, if the FBI and P.D. are satisfied, maybe you're overreacting and—"

"I'm not," Shawn said, cutting her off. "Make me a deal."

"Okay," she said since she felt like she really didn't have a choice.

"Promise me that you will let my men watch you 24/7 until I get to the bottom of this."

24/7.... Was he crazy? "Shawn, I don't think that's necessary."

"Promise me," he said in a stricter voice. She studied his face for any sign that he would drop the around-the-clock security idea and concluded that she was wasting her time.

"Okay," she said with a sigh. "I promise."

Chapter 17

"Shawn, is this really necessary?" Cyd asked him for the third time that day. Since returning to Chicago last week, Shawn had been accompanying Cyd everywhere. News had broken out about Jim Pearson, Paul Jensen, Bob Noland and a few others the day after they'd returned to Chicago. The FBI was credited for being a key part in demolishing the huge drug operation, and the identity of the woman who'd almost been kidnapped remained a mystery to the public. Agent Wolfe informed Shawn that he should be elated that the entire operation was destroyed and a case that had been open for the past three years was finally closed. The damage that was done in the cities of Detroit and Chicago was far from over after it was uncovered just how many individuals were involved with Leon Roberts. At least convicting Jim Pearson and Bob Noland was a huge plus and had exposed many layers of the drug operation.

Nonetheless, Shawn couldn't quite pinpoint why he still felt the need to follow Cydney. She thought he was crazy, and from the looks he'd been receiving from Micah, he believed he was crazy, too. At least Micah's brother Malik obliged his request and opened his search to other employees at the Peter Vallant Company. He couldn't shake the feeling that he hadn't found out if Jim had another inside source.

"Shawn, are you listening to me?" Cydney asked when they reached the front door of her parents' house.

"I'm sorry, what did you say?"

She gave him a look of irritation and placed one hand on her hip. "I said that Sunday brunch is very important for my family. My mom and partners will probably throw questions at you left and right about our relationship. Make sure your answers are concise and to the point, especially with my mother. You don't want to stumble over your words and give her ammo to use against us. Understood?"

"Of course," Shawn said as Cydney rang the doorbell. "But you make it seem like we're going to battle. It's just brunch, right?"

Cydney gave him a look of frustration. "No, it's not just brunch. If you say the wrong thing, my mother will have planned our wedding and named our kids before the day is over."

"Yeah, right," Shawn said with a laugh. "She can't be that bad."

Cyd smacked her lips and shook her head. "I love her dearly, but don't say I didn't warn you." The minute Cydney finished her statement, the door opened and Hope Rayne, Cydney's mother, wrapped her in a big hug.

"Mom, I'm okay, really."

"I know, but I still needed to hug you."

"Mom, you came to see me the day after I got back to Chicago."

"And I haven't seen you since then," Hope replied as she moved to let them in the door.

"Hello, Mrs. Rayne," Shawn said as he leaned in to hug her.

"How are you, Shawn?" she asked with a smile before leaning in to give him a hug.

"Crazy busy since every day I have to convince your daughter to let me protect her."

"She may be stubborn, but I don't want you to let her out of your sight."

"I won't, ma'am," Shawn said, returning her hug and greeting Mr. Rayne, who had walked over to shake his hand. Shawn hadn't seen her parents since Daman and Imani's wedding, but he felt as comfortable around them as he felt with Mama Jessie and Papa Willie.

Shawn followed Mr. and Mrs. Rayne into the living room where Cydney was giving hugs to her partners.

"Hey, man," Daman said as he slapped hands with Shawn.

"Hey, man, how are you?"

"Good, now that my sister-in-law is safe. Imani was freaking out when I told her what happened."

"I figured," Shawn said, stealing another glance in Cydney's direction. "It was a scary moment for me, too."

"Yeah, I can imagine," Daman stated. "Having the woman you love almost kidnapped not once, but twice. That's scary for any man."

"Exactly," Shawn replied, only hearing part of Daman's comment.

"Oh, so you do love her?" Daman asked.

"Wait, what?" Shawn replied while shaking his head. "Did you ask if I love her?"

Daman shook his head and laughed. "Man, you're usually more alert than this. Does Cyd know?"

Shawn looked from Daman to Cydney, then back to Daman again. The way he saw it, he had two options—either deny the truth or admit he had feelings for her. Neither option suited him at the moment.

"Don't worry, I won't say anything," Daman said, slapping him on the back. "If it's any consolation, I think she feels the same way."

"Really?" he asked, although he hadn't meant to sound so eager.

"Yeah, really," Daman replied, laughing once more. "I know how you feel. My love for Imani sneaked up the same way. One minute, you think you're just having sex with an incredible woman and enjoying her company. And the next, you realize that no woman you ever meet after her will compare or make you feel complete. Next thing ya know, you're down on one knee proposing."

"Naw, man," Shawn said, waving his hands in front of him. "Cydney will definitely expect more than a knee proposal. She'd want the works. You know, something to tame that spontaneous side she has."

Daman gave Shawn a look of confusion. "You do realize that you basically just admitted to the fact that you're ready to propose to her, right?"

Shawn glanced back over at Cydney and shook his head. "Damn," he said with a chuckle. "When the hell did that happen?"

"Oh, sweetie," Mrs. Rayne said as she touched his shoulder with her hand. "Love just has a way of sneaking up on you."

Shawn turned his head at the sound of Mrs. Rayne's

voice before he turned to Daman, who was sipping his untouched soda and masking a laugh.

"Um…Mrs. Rayne, I… Um…"

"Don't worry, sweetie," she said, giving him another squeeze and winking at Daman. "I won't tell her anything. It's best if she hears how you feel about her directly from you. But if you need my advice on when and where to propose, Daman can give you my cell number."

"Sweetie, how about we set the table for brunch?" David Rayne, Cydney's father, asked with a smile on his face as he led his wife away from Shawn and Daman.

"You've done it now, son," Mr. Rayne said for Shawn's ears only. "Welcome to the family."

A few seconds later Shawn was still standing there with a stunned look on his face while Daman laughed harder than he had since their arrival. Even the women looked over to see what was going on. Cydney gave Shawn a look of confusion and waved her hand toward the direction of her mom, who was walking out of the room with her dad with an extra pep in her step. Shawn didn't know what to tell her so he rose up his hands in defeat and mouthed *sorry.* Cyd's eyes got bigger as she mouthed *I warned you* before turning back to talk with the women.

Mrs. Rayne popped her head into the living room and asked Shawn to help her set the table. When he didn't answer quickly enough she flashed a smile and asked him again. As he made his way to Mrs. Rayne, he heard Daman's voice behind him.

"Enjoy the talk with your future mother-in-law," Daman said with a chuckle.

Shawn was about to comment, but Mrs. Rayne stuck her head back in the living room before he could. "I heard that, Daman," she said as she pointed her fingers to her eyes before pointing at his eyes. "I'm recruiting you to help me clean up after brunch so you can explain how long you plan on making me wait before you give me some grandkids."

"Aha," Shawn said as he laughed and pointed at Daman before going into the dining room to help Mrs. Rayne.

"Shawn is sexy," said Lex.

"I agree," stated Mya. The women had escaped to the upstairs den so that they could talk and gossip without any interruptions.

"Ladies," Cyd said, getting the attention of Lex, Mya and Imani. "I think I've really fallen hard for this man."

"Oh, sis, we already know that," Imani said as she waved her hand in the air. "The two of you have barely stopped looking at one another the entire day. And Mom and Dad are on cloud nine."

"Yeah, I can tell they like him," Cyd responded.

"Like him?" Imani said in a surprised voice. "Have you forgotten how many crazy antics you usually get yourself into? All the times you've unexpectedly left the country without warning just because you felt like it? Shawn's an FBI agent and Mom and Dad love the fact that he seems to keep you more grounded."

"I didn't need to be more grounded," Cyd retaliated.

"Oh, yes, you did," Lex interjected. "Need we remind you about the mess you recently got yourself into? Following a man who turned out to be a dangerous criminal?"

Whoops! They have me there. "Okay, but that's over now."

"Because your knight in shining armor saved you," Mya responded.

"Twice," Lex added.

"Geesh," Cyd said as she slunk down into the sofa chair a little. "You almost get kidnapped twice and no one lets you forget it."

All three women just gave her blank stares. "I'm kidding, guys," Cyd said with a laugh before sitting upright in her chair again. "Tough room."

"You scared the crap out of us," Imani said. "But we don't just like Shawn because he saved you. We also like Shawn because as complicated as you are sometimes, he understands you and lets you be yourself."

Cydney looked down at her hands before looking back at the women. "I know," Cyd replied. "He understands me more than I understand myself sometimes. And I understand him, too, and connect with him way past an intimate level."

"So what about your list?" Lex asked. "I think I remember you stating a few of the attributes that you needed for Mr. Right, and if I remember the Mr. Wrong list, Shawn's career definitely puts him at the top of that list."

"Yeah, you're right," Cyd said with a sigh. "But while we were cooped up in the cabin I started to realize that although he may not be perfect, he's definitely perfect for me," she continued, quoting Gamine's diary.

"And that's all that really matters, sis," Imani said as she gently squeezed Cyd's hand.

"So," Lex said as she curled her feet Indian-style on the couch. "You have to tell us about this cabin hideout with Shawn. We've been dying to know what it's like to be in witness protection with a man like that."

"Oh, this is definitely something I can tell you all about," Cyd said with a laugh, as the women got comfortable so they could listen to all the juicy details.

Just as she was about to start the story, Shawn popped his head in the den.

"Sorry to interrupt, ladies, but, Cydney, can I talk to you for a minute?"

"Um, sure," she said, looking from her partners to Shawn. Each woman had a look of interest in her eyes, wondering why he needed her at that particular moment.

Shawn waited until she was in the hallway to talk to her. "I just had a three-way call with Agent Wolfe and Peter Vallant. Due to all the bad media that the Peter Vallant Company has been associated with, Mr. Vallant still wants to have a final formal ball here in Chicago to wrap up the appreciation tour. He decided to pass out awards to the top contributors as well, so he'll need both events combined. And he still wants you to lead the planning, although he said he would understand if you don't feel up to it."

Cyd let out a big sigh, not prepared for what Shawn had just said. "Well, I guess since all the other events were canceled, it's not fair that Mr. Vallant's company has to suffer because of the recent course of events. What do you think?"

He lightly touched her cheek before he spoke. "I think that it's your decision, but know that me and my security team will definitely be there during the entire ball. I don't want you to think you're alone in this."

"We're all here," Imani said as she stepped out into the hallway with Lex and Mya right on her heels.

"We will be at the ball, too, sweetie," her dad said, standing next to her mom and Daman at the end of the stairs. Cyd followed Shawn's eyes as he looked around at her family members with slight disbelief.

"We don't keep many secrets in this family," Mrs. Rayne said in response to his confused look.

"I'm beginning to see that," he said, smiling at Mrs. Rayne before he turned his attention back to Cyd.

"One of us could also oversee this event," Imani added.

"No, that's okay," she said, looking at her sister before her eyes landed back on Shawn. "With your security team and all my family and friends around me, I should be fine at the event and it will be easy to plan, depending on how much time I have. When did Mr. Vallant want to reschedule the final event?"

"He was interviewed by the *Chicago Tribune* yesterday and told them that he would be having a formal right after Thanksgiving."

"Okay, that gives me about a week and a half," Cyd said as she clamped her hands together. She didn't know why, but she couldn't shake the uneasy feeling she had in the pit of her stomach. "Then I guess I have a lot of work to do before then."

"We'll put some of our projects on hold and help with this event," Imani said as she went to her sister and gave her a quick hug.

"Don't worry," Shawn said as he gave her a hug right after Imani. "I'll be right by your side every step of the way. Just breathe," he continued while holding her close to his heart as her suddenly quickened breaths started to subside.

Cyd noticed her mom lean into her dad as they watched the scene unfold between her and Shawn. She buried her face in his chest before looking up at him and giving him a peck on the lips that quickly turned more intimate. After that kiss, her family would definitely be more suspicious of her relationship with Shawn, although in that moment, she didn't care. She'd needed his kiss more than ever.

"Okay, ladies," Cyd said, clapping her hands together and trying to liven up the mood. "Shall we continue our conversation?" She looked toward her partners, who excitedly nodded their heads.

Her parents and Daman made their way back downstairs and eventually, Shawn followed suit. When she was at the doorway of the den and he'd descended a few stairs, he looked up at her and gave her a half smile. She returned his half smile and softly bit her bottom lip. Even from a distance, she could see the desire build in his eyes before he turned and walked down the rest of the stairs.

As she sat with the ladies and began telling them her story, she thought about her reaction to planning the formal awards ceremony for the Peter Vallant Company. She'd definitely underestimated how much the situation had affected her, but she had a great event to plan and she wasn't letting anything stand in the way of planning a successful one. Besides, there happened to be a lot of people in her corner who were willing to keep her safe. And with Agent Shawn Miles by her side, and in her heart, she felt safer than she'd felt in her entire life.

Chapter 18

After almost two weeks of restless nights and extensive planning, Cyd and the staff of Elite Events, Incorporated had worked day and night to bring the Peter Vallant Company Formal Awards Ceremony to life. She was exhausted, but she'd wanted everything to be as close to perfect as it could be, given the bad press that the Peter Vallant Company had received because of Jim Pearson. But luckily the company also had extremely loyal clients and contributors who RSVP'd despite it all.

Cyd gave herself a once-over in the hotel room mirror, pleased with her choice to wear an elegant black floor-length gown and stylish black stilettos with only earrings for accessories. Her hair was pulled to the side with soft curls flowing over her right shoulder and pinned with a delicate Swarovski crystal clip. She took out her blueberry lipstick to retouch her original application when she heard the hotel door open.

"You look absolutely stunning," Shawn said as he entered the room and walked straight toward her, pulling her into his embrace.

"And you look extremely sexy, Agent Miles," she

said as she gave him a quick peck on the lips, careful not to mess up her second application. Shawn had gotten a fresh haircut and trimmed his goatee, giving him a very clean-shaven look. It was hard not to want to sex the man senseless when he wore a classic black tuxedo and fashionable dress shoes, enhancing his natural sex appeal.

Shawn stepped back to admire the entire length of her outfit, his sea-blue eyes piercing through her and igniting the fire between her center. "I'm a lucky man," he said as he pulled her back to him and planted a hard kiss on her lips. Within seconds, she forgot all about the fact that she was trying not to mess up her lipstick.

They'd been spending every waking minute together since they'd left Tennessee and although they hadn't had a conversation about officially being in a relationship, it was a proved fact between their friends and family that they were definitely an item. It wasn't in either of their characters to have an official conversation confirming their relationship since with them, words had never been necessary.

On occasion, they introduced one another as boyfriend and girlfriend, but Shawn hadn't said the three magic words that Cyd longed to hear. Quite frankly, she worried that given his past, he was afraid to express his love to her for fear that something would happen to her. She honestly couldn't blame him since that fact had unfortunately been proved true with his parents and TJ.

"Was everything okay while I was gone?" Shawn asked, although he'd only been away from the room for thirty minutes.

"Let's see," Cyd said as she curled her arms around his neck. "You have two guards at my door and every five minutes they knock to see if I'm okay. Don't you think you're going a little overboard with this 24/7 watch idea?"

"Absolutely not," Shawn said as he placed sweet kisses along her collarbone. "There's no such thing as too much protection."

Cyd put her hands on her hips and gave him a look of disbelief. "Seriously!"

He didn't say anything, but he crossed his arms over his chest and observed her stance. *Crap, he always likes it when I stand this way.*

"I need you to focus," Cyd said as she took a few steps back from him. "Forget I asked the question. Let's just head to the formal."

"Um…no," he said firmly. "You know how I get when you put your hands on your hips like that." When her back hit the wall, she had nowhere else to go.

Just like that, she felt the sexual tension in the room rise to a higher level. She gazed into his eyes and realized he was at the point of no return. Shawn took another step closer to her and continued his original mission by placing wet kisses on her neck before his lips and tongue ventured to the top of her breasts.

"Shawn, we have to get to the ballroom for the formal," she said again, more breathlessly than before. Her words only made him kiss her quicker and in more places. His hands bunched her gown in his fists before they walked up her thighs, one hand pushing her panties aside and landing on her essence. Her thigh lifted on its own accord, landing in the palm of his hand at the same time that he stuck one of his fingers from his free hand precisely in her core. There, he moved his finger in and out until she was wet to his satisfaction.

Then he added another finger, playing with her clit at the same time.

"Shawn..." She moaned when she felt herself shiver at the sign that a strong orgasm was right around the corner. She gripped his neck tighter as he took his finger completely out before dipping back into her dripping-wet core. After a few more tweaks of his fingers, she released a forceful orgasm, crying into the ceiling as she did. Only then did she release her grip on his neck.

Shawn grabbed a piece of cloth out his pocket and dabbed her center clean. "Hmm, maybe I should take a quick shower," she said when she noticed remnants of her juices on his hands.

"You don't need one," Shawn said as he licked his fingers clean. "Most of your juices are on my hand. Besides," he continued. "I plan on finishing what I started after the formal and after I'm finished with you, you'll definitely need a shower."

"Point taken," Cyd said as she sashayed to the bathroom to freshen up. After ten minutes of washing up and refreshing her makeup, they were finally ready to head to the formal. As they walked into the ballroom, Cyd admired the great work her and her team had done. The simple, yet classy, decorations definitely made a statement and Mr. Vallant had expressed his utmost gratitude for everything she and her team had accomplished on such short notice.

A lot of the attendees were still arriving, but her parents and partners had arrived early.

"Cydney, I'd like to officially introduce you to my partner, Micah Madden," Shawn said as Micah extended his hand. Of course, Cyd already knew who he was, but she'd never been introduced to him properly.

"I'm going to survey the premises," Shawn said as he kissed her cheek. "I'll be back as soon as I can."

"Okay," Cyd said as she resumed conversing with her family. Ten minutes into the conversation, she excused herself to check with the caterer. She'd only taken a few steps before she noticed Micah hot on her tail. She ignored him at first and continued toward the kitchen. After her conversation with the caterer, she walked over to Mr. Vallant and the executive team to make sure they knew their speaking order for the awards portion of the night.

"Did you need something?" she asked, although she had a pretty good idea why he was still following her. Micah just looked at her and offered a quick smile before his face turned stoic again.

"Seriously," she said, crossing her arms over her chest. "Even during tonight's event, Shawn wants someone watching me at all times. I thought I only needed to be watched before and after the formal ceremony?"

"I'm just following orders," Micah said, as if that answered everything.

"Sure you are," Cyd said as she let out a frustrated breath. "Look, I still have to talk with a couple contributors who are presenting their success stories to the crowd in an hour. Can you do me a favor and actually say something when I approach them?"

"What do you want me to say?" Micah asked.

"I don't know," Cyd said as she wailed her arms. "I know you're usually more lively than this, so how about you actually introduce yourself this time?"

"I can do that," Micah said right before she met the next group.

"Hi, I'm Micah," Micah said awkwardly as she approached everyone. *Could he sound more monotone?* Cyd thought as she shot him a look of irritation. She figured Shawn must have told him to act professional because she'd definitely seen Micah more relaxed. After she finished speaking with the group, she tracked down her sister, Imani, and brother-in-law, Daman.

"Daman, do you know Micah?"

"Uh, yes," Daman said as if he could tell she was fishing for something.

"Great! I need you to tell him to back off." Cyd watched Daman and Micah share a head nod before he answered her with a solid, "No!" Imani began laughing until Cyd shot her a death stare that made her stop laughing instantly.

Cyd glanced over at Micah, who was now wearing a smug look on his face. *This is going to be a long night,* she thought as she grabbed a glass of wine from one of the passing waiters.

"Malik, this is Shawn. Have you found anything yet?" Shawn asked from inside a secure room down the hallway from the main hotel ballroom.

"Not yet," Malik said on the other line. "I haven't seen any red flags, but I'm still making it through the second list you gave me. So far everyone's been clean."

"Dang, okay," Shawn said as he shook his head. Waiting for Malik to find something when there may be nothing left to find was truly an agonizing process. "Man, call me if anything changes."

"I always do."

Shawn hung up the phone and reminded a few of his security men to make sure they kept their eyes open. The FBI and P.D. were no longer involved in the case since they'd already resolved what they needed to solve or conclude in the resolution of the case. Truth be told, he didn't think that either government team even cared about Cydney's safety since so many people involved were already behind bars.

Shawn made his way down the hallway to the main ballroom. "Hey, Micah," he said, tapping him on his shoulder. "We're switching positions."

Cydney turned at the sound of his voice and lifted one eyebrow. "If it isn't Prince Charming here to relieve his loyal follower," she said in a sarcastic voice. Evidently, she didn't think she needed protection during the formal ceremony. Micah mouthed *good luck* before leaving the ballroom.

From the way she was glaring at him, he was going to need a whole lot of luck. She was an independent woman in every sense of the word, so he knew this was hard for her. "Well, rest assured that the way I plan on protecting you will be a helluva lot better than Micah," he whispered, briefly kissing her behind her ear.

"Is that a promise?" she asked, softening the hard defense exterior she'd apparently built upon learning she wouldn't go anywhere at the formal without an escort. "I missed you," she said as she played with the collar of his shirt. Shawn was in the middle of his response when he noticed her looking past his shoulders at something that had gotten her attention.

He glanced over his shoulder and spotted Brittany Higgins walking into the event way past fashionably late.

"Don't worry about her," he said when he turned back to Cydney. "By now she's probably heard that we're dating."

"Is that all we're doing?" Cydney asked him questionably.

"No, that's not all we're doing," Shawn answered, realizing that the sight of Brittany had made her uneasy. "You're the only woman for me, Cydney." He gently grabbed the bottom of her chin. "I can't imagine being with anyone else." Although he'd realized he loved and wanted to spend the rest of his life with her before they'd left the cabin, he didn't feel like now was the best time to tell her.

"Do you mean that?" she asked as she searched his eyes for confirmation.

"Absolutely," he said as he leaned down to give her a kiss, not caring that there were many onlookers and people from the media there to witness the moment. By the time they stopped kissing, he'd had his Cydney back. *His.* He loved the sound of that.

Mr. Vallant walked over after the kiss. "You know," he said, slapping Shawn on the back. "I have a rule against people dating in my company. But I guess since you both are contract employees with tonight being your last day, I'll make an exception." The three of them shared a laugh.

"That was some kiss," Kim Lathers said to Shawn and Cydney after Mr. Vallant left.

"Oh, man, that was hot," said Verona, joining them, as well. "And, Cydney," Verona said as she opened her purse and moved around a few things before pulling out a black bracelet. "Before I forget, I found this in the bathroom. Isn't this yours?"

"Yes, it is, thank you," Cydney exclaimed before studying the piece and sliding it back on her wrist.

Shawn watched Cydney search the room, apparently searching for someone.

"I never did understand women and purses," Shawn said to try to distract Cydney as he watched Verona struggle to stuff a few contents back into her clutch. Shawn knew who Cydney was searching for because he was trying to find the same person.

"Men don't need to understand," Cydney said as both women joined her in laughter. Once Cydney was engaged in a conversation with the women, Shawn finally spotted Brittany and detected that she wasn't too happy with their open display of affection. She was at the bar with a drink in her hand, glaring at them from across the room.

"Did you see the look on Brittany's face after y'all kissed?" Kim asked Cydney.

"Not really," Cydney responded.

"Goodness," Kim exclaimed. "She practically burned a hole straight through you guys," she said to Shawn and Cydney as Verona nodded her head in agreement. *Maybe I really shouldn't have flirted back at her,* Shawn thought, although he couldn't change the past now. But he definitely knew he had to keep his eye on Brittany. She originally hadn't been on his radar, but now that he thought about it, no one was ruled out.

"She makes me feel uncomfortable," Cydney exclaimed after Kim and Verona left.

"Ignore her," Shawn said as he led her to another corner of the room. He didn't need Cydney concerning herself with Brittany, but as always, something definitely didn't feel right to him. There was something in the air…something that was making him uncomfortable, too. He didn't want to worry Cydney, but he felt like he was missing a very important detail of the puzzle. Although everyone thought he was paranoid, his gut had never steered him wrong. *Time's running out, Miles,* he thought. With the event coming to a close, it was going to be even harder to figure out if there was anyone else after Cydney, but he knew he wouldn't stop until his gut established that she was safe.

Chapter 19

"Thank you so much for everything," Mr. Vallant said with appreciation as he extended his hand. The lines of stress that had frequented his forehead lately had not been present the entire night.

"You're very welcome," Cyd responded sincerely, returning his handshake. Mr. Vallant and a few of the last attendees walked out of the ballroom and expressed their gratitude for a great night. The final event of the appreciation tour had been a huge success and the awards ceremony to honor top contributors had been a great addition to the formal. With the exception of Brittany Higgins, who'd stormed out of the ballroom shortly after her and Shawn's public kiss, everything had gone smoothly.

"Do you need help with anything?" Imani asked.

"I'm fine, sis," Cyd replied as she gave her a hug. "I just need to make sure the hotel sales manager doesn't need anything else from me."

"Okay, we'll be at the house," Imani said as she motioned for her partners and Daman to follow her. Her parents had retired early and the rest of them were going

Sherelle Green   197

to Imani and Daman's estate for drinks to celebrate another successful event.

Cyd wrapped up the final details with the sales manager while the hotel staff continued to clean the ballroom.

"Are you ready to head out?" Shawn asked, with Micah close behind.

"Yes, I'm ready," she said, holding her clutch and taking one last glance at the ballroom to make sure they didn't leave anything behind.

Cyd was so relieved that the appreciation tour was officially over. It had been way more intense than she'd originally prepared for, but planning such a huge series of events was definitely great for her company.

When they reached the lobby, the wine and water she'd been drinking all night was finally catching up to her. She was so busy she'd been holding her bladder the entire night and that definitely wasn't healthy. "Shawn, I have to go to the bathroom before we leave."

"Um, okay. I'll go with you?"

Cyd stopped short. "You mean you'll wait here in the lobby while I go to the bathroom, right?"

"No, I mean I will wait in the bathroom with you. I just won't go in the stall." *Goodness, is he for real?*

"Come on, Shawn. I've been real accommodating all night," she said.

"Aha, yeah, right," Micah chimed in with a laugh.

"Zip it," she said to Micah, laughing along with him. "I promise to be quick and besides, how will you explain your presence to the women who go in and out of the bathroom?" She waved her hands around the lobby at all the women present to validate her point.

Shawn gave her an uneasy look before doing a 360

around the crowded lobby. Most of the attendees who'd left the formal had settled at the bar. "Okay, I won't go in the bathroom, but I'm definitely waiting right outside the door."

"Deal," Cyd agreed as she headed to the bathroom to release her bladder.

"Hello," she said to a woman who was exiting the bathroom.

"Hi," the woman replied before leaving. There was one stall that was occupied, a couple that were a little unclean and another that would have to do. After Cyd washed her hands, she took out her lipstick to reapply a fresh coat just as the other occupied stall opened.

"Hey," Cyd said to the familiar face that walked out of the stall.

"Hey yourself, princess," said the other female in an icy voice right before Cyd felt the solid poke of something hard on her side. "If you try to scream or say anything, I'll shoot you quicker than you can voice one word."

Cyd looked at her through the mirror, her heart beating so fast that she was sure she would have a panic attack at any moment. *Is she serious?*

"Aw, does that look mean you're confused as to why I'd want to hurt you?" the woman said as she yanked Cyd's head backward by grabbing a fistful of hair. Cyd almost yelped at the sharp pain that shot through her neck at the forceful snatch, but she thought about the woman's threatening words. "I'm here to finish the job that my partners clearly couldn't finish. And mark my words, princess," she said as she pushed the hard object even more into Cyd's side. "I won't mess up like they did."

Cyd stared into her eyes to see if she could see any signs of empathy, but saw nothing in her eyes but amusement. She was enjoying this. *Oh, I knew I got a weird vibe from this woman!* The woman yanked her hair a little more before pointing to the window.

Shawn, where are you? Cyd thought as she was forced to stand on the sink and climb through one bathroom window while the woman climbed out of the other at the same time. *Should I just scream and call her bluff?* It seemed like a good idea, but Cyd was certain that she would be shot if she didn't follow directions.

"Walk," the woman said in a mighty voice as she waved her hand toward the alley. At one point, Cyd thought about tackling the woman to the ground, since she was taller than she was by at least a few inches. But the woman had her by at least forty pounds. *Come on, Shawn, where are you?* She had no idea how to get herself out this situation and before she had a chance to formulate any more thoughts, she was knocked out cold.

"Nobody move!" a woman yelled at the top of her lungs as she hopped on a table in the lobby wearing a wedding veil, white party dress and no heels. "If you do, I'm liable to hurt anyone who crosses my path." People in the lobby and bar gasped in surprise at the crazy woman on top of the table. A quick observation of her hands proved she didn't have a weapon. Suddenly, she did a little happy dance while singing "Happy Birthday."

"Hahahaha, just kidding," the woman said as she tried to get off the table and was instantly surrounded by girls wearing T-shirts with the word *bridesmaid* written on it. *Man, I hate that stuff,* Shawn thought as he reflected on a previous time where he'd been on high alert just to find out that the sneaky-looking women were actually participating in bachelorette party antics.

Shawn looked at Micah and nodded for him to check out the scene, anyway. *Cydney,* he thought when he realized she hadn't come out of the bathroom. He knocked before peeking his head in.

"Cydney," he called, but received no answer. He walked completely into the bathroom and instantly noticed the open windows.

"Crap," he said as he hopped on the sink and peered out the window down both ways of the alley. Nothing. Not a single person. Before running out of the bathroom, he pushed open each door just to make sure she wasn't in there and didn't find anyone. But he did find a scarf.

"Micah," Shawn yelled as he ran up to his partner who was now surrounded by the bride and bridesmaids.

"Shawn, what's wrong?" Micah asked in concern.

"Someone got to her," Shawn whispered in his ear. "We have to move ASAP!"

"Oh, crap," Micah said as he quickly discarded his tie and handed it to one of the women.

"Why are you giving her that?"

"The bride has a list of things she has to accomplish before midnight and her time is almost up."

Shawn shook his head and made his way toward the hotel desk to inform security. As Shawn and Micah ran out the front entrance, Shawn heard someone from the bridal group state that she was so glad she'd gotten the list from a strange woman. Something clicked.

"Who did you get this list from?" Shawn asked the group as he backtracked a couple feet.

"Some lady," one of the bridesmaids said. Shawn took the lipstick-written list from the bride's hand and noticed that the list had specific times and places to do everything, including getting a piece of clothing from the first man who helped her off the table.

"How long ago did you get this?"

"I got it, actually," said another bridesmaid who was standing off to the side. "I'm the maid of honor and I just got it when I went in the bathroom. I was hanging up the phone with my sister and expressing how I needed to spice up the bachelorette party. This woman jotted something down for me real quick and I showed the ladies the list." Shawn studied the bridesmaid's face and remembered her walking out of the bathroom just as Cydney had entered.

"Do you remember how she looked?" he asked the bridesmaid.

"Not really," the bridesmaid said, obviously a little taken off guard by all the questions. "She was wearing that scarf you have in your hand and all her body parts were covered."

Shawn wanted to ask them more questions but everyone in the group had obviously been drinking so he was lucky he'd been told anything at all.

"Let's head to the alley," Shawn yelled to Micah. "Call the team and tell them to talk with the security guards at the hotel. They don't have cameras inside the bathroom, but I noticed a camera that was pointed in the direction of the bathroom, so we should be able to see who went in and never came out."

As Micah made the call to the team, Shawn called Malik.

"They took her again," Shawn said into the phone

as he and Micah arrived at the empty alley. "And since they captured her in the women's bathroom, a witness confirmed there was another woman in there with Cydney. Anything on the other employees?"

"I'm only through searching everyone with a last name that begins with *L*. As far as the woman in the company who interacted with Cydney, Brittany Higgins is clean. So is Kim Lathers."

"Damn," Shawn said as he massaged his forehead. "What am I missing?"

"You're too personally involved," Micah said as he entered the conversation. "Take a step back and think."

Shawn did as Micah suggested and passed his phone over to Micah, who began talking with Malik. He walked over to the side wall of the building and began thinking.

Okay, it's definitely a woman. More than likely, a Peter Vallant employee who interacted with her. Suddenly, his mind went to his time earlier with Cydney when they were in the hotel room. "Bad timing," he said quietly to himself as he thought about his hands roaming up and down her body, landing on her butt and caressing her breasts.

Focus, Miles, he said quietly to himself, but his mind was still remembering the intimate moment between them in the hotel room. He leaned his head back on the wall and closed his eyes. He let his mind wander back to their time in the hotel room, since his gut had never steered him wrong. In his memory, he was on the outside observing the scene as their foreplay unfolded before him. He witnessed Cydney as she lifted her leg and he saw himself grab her leg to keep her steady. He watched himself stick his finger inside her as she dropped her head back in satisfaction. He could hear the moans escape her mouth as the passion overtook her body. He witnessed her release her orgasm in an explosion of desire before coming back down to earth, and he could see himself arch his back to plunge even deeper as her juices flowed over his hand.

As his eyes remained closed he watched Cydney give him a seductive smile as she unlatched her arms from around his neck. And that was when he saw it. That was when he noticed the one detail he'd wished he'd recognized hours sooner. There, as clear as ever, he noticed that both of her wrists were bare...clear of all accessories.

"How did I miss that?" Shawn said aloud and he ran back over to Micah and grabbed the phone out of his hand. "Malik, I know who it is, I know who took Cydney."

"Who?" Malik asked on the line at the same time Micah asked in person.

"Verona Neely," Shawn said to them both. "Malik, I need you to find everything you can on Verona Neely immediately!"

"Right away," Malik said, hanging up the phone.

"How do you know?" Micah asked in confusion as to how Shawn had just come up with Verona as the person of interest seemingly out of the blue. Shawn placed his hand on his forehead again. He'd just thought of another detail.

"Earlier today, Verona gave Cydney a bracelet that she claimed Cydney left in the bathroom. But I finally remember from earlier that Cydney wasn't wearing a bracelet tonight. Matter of fact, Cydney was looking at the bracelet funny, but she was too distracted by Brittany Higgins to question anything. We both were. And now I remember seeing something that was black and leather sticking out of Verona's purse when she took out the bracelet. I'd bet any amount of money that those gloves are biker gloves."

"You think she's the owner of those motorcycle tracks we found back in Springfield?" Micah asked, finally catching on.

"Definitely," Shawn said as he took out his phone to call Agent Wolfe. Although Malik was on the case, he needed to call the FBI in case Cydney's disappearance was related to anything else currently going on in the city.

"I understand, sir," Shawn said in response to Agent Wolfe's orders to stand down until he could send the team out there. "But with all due respect, tonight I'm not an FBI agent." He glanced over at Micah, who was listening intently. "Tonight I'm just a man trying to save the woman he loves."

Chapter 20

Shawn paced the entire length of the security room as he awaited a call from Malik and the return of Micah and another agent who'd gone to Verona's apartment. He'd called Daman, who had brought Cydney's parents and sister back to the hotel after they'd heard the news. Agent Wolfe was also present in the room and Shawn's security team, along with two FBI agents and friends, were discreetly patrolling inside and outside the hotel for clues. Although Agent Wolfe often went by the book, he'd dropped protocol when Shawn had expressed his love for Cydney.

Cydney had been missing for two hours and Shawn couldn't believe he had let someone get to her again. *I knew I should have followed her into the bathroom,* he thought for the hundredth time since the incident.

Shawn stopped pacing and sat in the chair to try to calm his nerves. No such luck. Mrs. Rayne gave him a look of sympathy, but he saw the pain in her eyes from holding back remaining tears and frustration from unanswered questions. Shawn had spent the first hour she'd gone missing walking up and down the streets and alley trying to find any clues that would help them figure out where she was. He'd even thoroughly checked an abandoned building several times before he was forced to stop to explain the situation to Cydney's family when they'd arrived.

Shawn nodded his head toward Daman to indicate that they should continue the search when his phone rang.

"Hey, Malik, you're on speaker. What did you find out?"

"For starters, Verona Neely's real name is Victoria Noland, the daughter of Bob Noland, that fast-food-chain CEO who tried to kidnap Cydney in the first place."

"I never read anything about him having a daughter in the papers or online."

"You wouldn't," Malik added. "Looks like Victoria, or Verona, was kept out of the public's eye since Bob's family forbade him to have an illegitimate daughter with Verona's mother, an African-American woman. But I guess…like father, like daughter."

"Yeah, that makes sense," Shawn said, understanding a few more pieces of the puzzle.

"And guess who she's dating? Jim Pearson, of all people. His record is still pretty clean, so he probably got suckered into doing what the father-daughter duo wanted him to do when he joined the Peter Vallant Company."

"What about Mr. Vallant?" Shawn asked, glancing over at Agent Wolfe, who appeared to be holding his breath as he awaited news on his dear friend.

"No, he's clean," Malik confirmed.

"I'll call and inform the FBI on the other news,"

Agent Wolfe said as he went to the corner of the room to inform the FBI of the new developments in Jim Pearson's and Bob Noland's cases.

"That's all I was able to find in a couple hours, but I'm still researching and reaching out to a lot of contacts to piece together other red flags I've found. Once I learned that Verona Neely was really Victoria Noland, I uncovered a lot more. Looks like Bob somehow convinced her to put a lot of things in her name. I also called Micah since I knew he was at Verona's home and I needed him to check out something for me." Malik continued on the phone. Shawn was just about to request that Malik elaborate on what info he was researching about the Nolands when the door opened.

"I think I found what you're looking for, Malik," Micah said as he and the other agent entered the room.

"What did you find?" Shawn asked.

"Way more than we suspected," Micah replied as he opened his bag. "Besides the fact that Verona, or should I say Victoria, definitely led a double life, it looks like dear daddy leads a secret life, as well."

Micah opened his bag and took out a large file. "All the information in my bag was locked in a safe, but I cracked the code." He tossed the largest file toward Shawn.

"Lead Assassins Combat? What company is this?"

"Well, LAC, as it's stated on numerous files, is owned by Bob Noland, but most of the filed paperwork is in Victoria Noland's name."

Shawn flipped through the papers and looked questionably at Micah when he didn't respond right away.

"Malik, your suspicions were correct," Micah said to his brother on his phone. Malik let out an expletive.

"What?" Shawn asked Micah.

"Well, LAC is apparently a company you go to when you want to hire a hit man. Bob Noland's been in the business for almost thirty years and five months ago, his daughter joined him, although he'd been falsifying documents in her name for the past decade."

Shawn closed the file as the hair on the back of his neck stood on edge. *No way,* he thought as Malik handed him another file. Shawn skimmed through the file and page after page was filled with detailed accounts of the people who had contracted the LAC and their targets, starting with the most recent. His fingers began moving in slow motion as he got toward the end of the file. When he reached the last page, there were only five names listed as targets for that year. Even worse, that entire page listed Leon Roberts as the person who hired LAC. *Really! A drug dealer who hired a professional hit man?* Shawn's anger skyrocketed the more he studied the page.

"Why did they take Cydney?" Shawn all but yelled to Micah, who walked over to him and placed his hand on his shoulder.

"Why?" Shawn repeated as he closed the file and slammed it on a nearby table.

"What's going on?" Mr. Rayne asked in aggravation since most of the individuals in the room were in the dark about the situation.

"Sir, ma'am," Shawn said as he looked over to Cydney's parents. "According to the file, my parents were killed by someone at LAC twenty-nine years ago who was hired by Leon Roberts, a drug dealer I helped lock up three years ago. Since recently I helped bring down the entire operation, including the fall of Bob Noland, my guess is that his daughter wanted revenge and since she couldn't get to me…she decided to take Cydney."

Cydney's family gasped in shock and devastation at the news Shawn had disclosed.

"Shawn, that's not a proved fact," Malik said on the phone.

"I know," Shawn responded quickly although he felt partially to blame. Deep down, he knew he shouldn't blame himself. He'd always known that Leon was behind his parents' deaths and he was actually happy that he finally knew the truth. But he had no time to wallow in self-pity, although he did allow himself a quick second to relish in the relief that his parents' deaths were solved. He guessed that a deeper look into LAC would probably prove that TJ was a target, as well.

"Malik, can you pull up a list of all the properties Bob Noland owns?"

"Already done," Malik said over the phone. "I'm sending it to both your and Micah's phones now."

"Great," Shawn said as he opened the message on his Android. "Micah, take two security-team members and check the last two locations on the list. Agent Wolfe, you take an agent and check the middle one. And Daman," Shawn said as he made his way to the other side of the room, "we will take the first two."

"I'll stay here with my wife and daughter," Mr. Rayne said. "Oh, and Shawn," he continued as he walked over and gripped him on his shoulder. "I need you to bring my baby girl home safely."

"Sir," Shawn answered, momentarily glancing at Agent Wolfe. "You have my word that I will bring her back safely. I promise." He hugged Mrs. Rayne and whispered the same words into her ear, hoping they provided her with a little comfort.

Shawn looked at Agent Wolfe again as he nodded his head in approval. He knew he was breaking all kinds of protocols, but at the moment, all rules ceased to exist in his mind. There was no way he was losing another person in his life—absolutely no way.

Cyd lifted her head and opened her eyes, unaware of how long she'd been unconscious. The few sporadic lamps offered some visibility but no one appeared to be in the room with her. *Is this a warehouse?* she wondered, since the space she was in looked a little empty and almost like a large garage. She had no idea where she was or how Verona had managed to get her there, and the loud heavy-metal music that bounced off the walls sounded worse than nails on a chalkboard. The back of her head was still pounding in the spot that Verona had hit her, but she refused to close her eyes again. She had to be alert, and there was no doubt in her mind that Shawn was on his way to save her. She was confident of that.

Cyd tried to crack her back as she adjusted herself in the hard chair. She couldn't tell how her hands were tied, but she knew they were confined by plastic. She twisted her arm to try to squeeze her hands free.

"I wouldn't do that if I were you," Verona said as she walked out from a dark corner.

"Why are you doing this?" Cyd said, trying not to act as startled as she felt.

"Isn't it obvious?" Verona asked with a laugh. "You stuck your nose in where it didn't belong, just like your little boyfriend did a few years ago."

"What are you talking about?" Cyd asked, although now she was pretty sure Verona and Jim were working together.

"My dad told me to leave you alone, and so did Jim at one point. But honestly, I wanted to see if I could kidnap you and get away with it."

Cyd watched Verona as she began circling her. *Jim? Her dad? What is she talking about?*

"Bob Noland is my dad, by the way," Verona said. "And Jim and I have been dating for years, so all that time he was with you, he was doing it for me."

Cyd wanted to tell her that she could have that sorry excuse for a man, but she didn't want to say anything reckless. However, she couldn't help but ask a few questions.

"Verona, why did you have Jim pretend to be interested in me?"

"Ugh," she responded as she stomped around the room. "My name isn't Verona…it's Vic, short for Victoria."

"Okay," Cyd said in a calming voice. *Remember, Cyd, you can't argue with crazy,* she reminded herself, already concluding that Verona, or Vic, had lost her freaking mind.

"To answer your question, princess, I just wanted him to learn more about you. I love my baby, but he isn't the sharpest tool in the shed. Although going to jail for my plan was the smartest thing he's done since I met him."

Out of nowhere, Vic started dancing in circles and chanting that her dad would be so proud that she'd successfully kidnapped her first person.

"I can't believe he failed to kidnap you but I didn't!

I was pissed when Jim told me that others in our organization were targeting you, as well." Vic stopped twirling and crossed her arms in a pout. "You were my kidnapping, not theirs." Instead of continuing to dance, she slowly walked closer to Cyd.

What the heck is she doing? Cyd thought when Vic was mere inches from her face.

"I want to make sure I remember every detail about you in this exact moment," she said as she deeply inhaled and exhaled before stating that she even wanted to remember Cyd's scent. Cyd kept a solemn face, but inside, her nerves were jumping through hoops.

"I like the combination of lavender and vanilla," Cyd said with a discomforting laugh as she tried to get think of a way to get inside Vic's head. Vic let out a brief chuckle before her face grew serious and she took another breath. *Goodness, she looks creepy when she does that!*

"So," Vic said as she leaned over right in front of Cyd and flicked a hand through her hair. "I don't have anyone else to talk to, so what's the first thing you want to talk about before I start torturing you?"

Torture? Is this chick for real? Cyd thought as she glared up at her with mass confusion. *Oh, heck, no. I refuse to be killed by this crazy woman.* Between the sniffing, exhaling and the dancing, the situation was growing more irritating by the minute. Cyd wasn't demeaning the dangerousness of the situation, but she also thought if she had to die at an early age it would be in a situation a whole lot more exciting than a kidnapping by a crazy woman.

"Come on," Vic said in a whiny voice. "What do you want to talk about? I know," she stated as she snapped her fingers. "Let's talk about why I wanted to kidnap you in detail. Well, for starters, you always dressed way too nice."

Oh, come on!

"And *all* the men in the company liked you. That's really bruising to a girl's ego, you know?"

"And third, you're really slender so you were the easiest of the women to target and kidnap. Jim tried flirting with Brittany Higgins and Kim Lathers to get me my first kidnapping, but they wouldn't flirt back," Vic said as she crossed her arms over her chest and poked out her lips in a pout.

Lord, help me, Cyd thought as she listened to Vic rattle off insane reasons for wanting to kidnap her. *Okay, maybe I'll just close my eyes until she finishes.*

"And fourth, I…" Vic's voice trailed off and Cyd popped her eyes open again.

"You what?" Shawn said as he pressed the pistol into her side.

Oh, my goodness, thank you, thank you, she thought as she looked up toward the ceiling.

"Daman, untie Cydney," Shawn ordered as he handcuffed Vic.

"Brother-in-law, I'm so happy to see you," Cyd said as she stood up slowly and finally cracked her back.

"Me, too," he said as he gave her a big hug. "Let me call the police and then I'll call your sister and parents."

"Did you secure the premises?" Cyd asked, not knowing if there were more criminals in the warehouse.

Shawn gave her his best "what do you think" look before he started toward a door in the distance.

"Shawn, don't you know who I am?" Vic yelled as they made their way outside. Cyd looked around, sur-

prised to see that they were near a few office buildings
and a forest preserve. She could hear the police sirens
getting closer with each step they took.

"I'm a Noland," Vic said as she attempted to kick her
way out of his grip. "I wasn't going to hurt her. I only
wanted to pretend to complete my first kidnap. This
gave me such a bigger adrenaline rush than I got when
I helped the druggies use the mock Peter Vallant vans to
transport cocaine. With kidnapping, it's all about me."

Shawn shook his head in skepticism, not believing
that she was a bigger mole in the Peter Vallant Company
than Jim. "Just so you know," he said to Cyd. "We didn't
find any weapons in the warehouse…only a BB gun and
boxes of drugs that I'm sure will link back to the case."

Cyd's head whipped around to Vic. "A BB gun? Seriously? You kidnapped me with a freaking BB gun?"

Vic didn't say anything and just continued to laugh
hysterically. She was still laughing when the police arrived to take her off to jail.

A BB gun? Cyd thought again, still surprised that
she'd actually let someone kidnap her who didn't even
have a real gun. She leaned against a stationary police
car as she watched another police car take Vic into
custody.

"Are you still thinking about that BB gun?" Shawn
asked as he leaned on the car next to her.

"Of course I am," Cyd said as she waved her hands
in the air. "I can't believe I let her kidnap me with a
fake gun."

"Better a fake one than a real one," Shawn said in a
serious tone. When he gazed back at her, she noticed
the worry lines in his face.

"You know that my kidnapping wasn't your fault, don't you?"

After a couple seconds, he gave her a soft smile before he laughed. "After hearing the crazy explanation Vic gave you, yeah."

"Good," she said with a slight smile.

Her hair caught in the chilly wind and slashed across her face. Shawn tucked the tousled hair behind her ear. "You know, I was worried sick about you," he said as he pulled her a little closer to him.

"I know," she responded. "But I knew you would come for me."

"You were that confident?" Shawn asked as he searched her eyes for confirmation.

"Yes," she said, choosing her next words extremely carefully. "I figured if you loved me any fraction as much as I love you, there was no way you'd stop searching until I was found."

Shawn gave her a deep smile and softly pecked her lips before speaking. "I'm so glad to hear you say that because I happen to love you very, *very* much." He tightened his arms around her waist and stationed her right between the fit of his legs.

"Why, Agent Miles, I do believe you just professed your unyielding love for me. I could have sworn I was just another notch on your list of women."

"Not another notch," he said as his face grew serious. "You're the only notch, the only woman I want to spend the rest of my life with."

Cyd bit her lip and tried to hold back her huge smile. "Even if I tend to get myself into trouble sometimes?"

Shawn looked around at all the parked police cars, and listened to the sirens in the distance from a fire truck and ambulance that were still headed their way. "Yeah," he said with a laugh. "Because I can't imagine you getting into more trouble than this."

Cyd laughed along with him before bringing him closer to place a passionate kiss on his lips. "I love you," she said again, just because she liked the sound of those three words.

"I love you, too," he said as he placed a couple kisses along her neckline. Even the smallest peck on her neck brought her desire to a heightened level.

"Did you ever think one night in Anguilla would turn into love?" she asked out of curiosity.

"I didn't know it would turn into love, but I knew one night with you would never be enough. I thought about you every day after Anguilla."

Cyd touched her hand to his cheek and looked into his eyes. "I did, too—my mystery lover with the sea-blue eyes. But nothing could have prepared me for the real Shawn Miles, the man behind the mysterious mask." She let both hands settle on his chest. "The more I learned about you, the deeper I fell in love. You're it, Shawn.... You're my perfect man."

Cyd watched a slight mist fill his eyes before he pulled her in for a tight hug. He didn't say anything for a couple minutes and Cyd cradled his head to her shoulder, giving him a moment to soak in her words.

When he lifted his head and brought his face mere inches from hers, her heartbeat quickened as she studied his eyes. She didn't see any more secrets reflected in his gaze. Gone were the last of the barriers he'd set in place, and before her stood a man who not only deserved her love, but accepted it.

"So tell me something, Ms. Rayne. What does a man

have to do to get you to agree to be the future Mrs. Miles?" Shawn asked.

Cyd looked around at all the chaos that surrounded them and gave him a questioning look.

"What?" Shawn asked her in concern. "What's wrong?"

"Well," she said as she curled her arms around his neck. "Is this an official proposal?"

"Goodness, woman," he said with a laugh as he shook his head. "I warned Daman this would happen."

"Huh? Warned Daman about what?"

"You are something else," he said in his best Kevin Hart imitation as he shook his head in disbelief. "If you must know, this is not the way I plan to officially propose to you. But it is my way of getting an idea on what a man needs to do for a proper proposal that meets Cydney Rayne's standards."

She giggled and swayed back and forth in his arms. "For starters, I think you should seriously consider proposing where it all started!"

"I actually wanted to hear your ideas, but not the place. Now you'll know I'm proposing the next time we travel to Anguilla."

"Not if we go to Anguilla every couple months," she said with an innocent look on her face.

Shawn laughed as he placed a sweet kiss on her lips. "How did I get so lucky?"

She looked into his hypnotizing eyes and gave him a sneaky smile before responding. "I was just asking myself the same thing," she said. "How did you get so lucky?"

* * * * *

REQUEST YOUR FREE BOOKS!

2 FREE NOVELS
PLUS 2 FREE GIFTS!

KIMANI™
ROMANCE

Love's ultimate destination!

YES! Please send me 2 FREE Harlequin® Kimani™ Romance novels and my 2 FREE gifts (gifts are worth about $10). After receiving them, if I don't wish to receive any more books, I can return the shipping statement marked "cancel." If I don't cancel, I will receive 4 brand-new novels every month and be billed just $5.19 per book in the U.S. or $5.74 per book in Canada. That's a savings of at least 20% off the cover price. It's quite a bargain! Shipping and handling is just 50¢ per book in the U.S. and 75¢ per book in Canada.* I understand that accepting the 2 free books and gifts places me under no obligation to buy anything. I can always return a shipment and cancel at any time. Even if I never buy another book, the two free books and gifts are mine to keep forever.

168/368 XDN F4XC

Name	(PLEASE PRINT)
Address	Apt. #
City	State/Prov.	Zip/Postal Code

Signature (if under 18, a parent or guardian must sign)

Mail to the **Harlequin® Reader Service:**

IN U.S.A.: P.O. Box 1867, Buffalo, NY 14240-1867
IN CANADA: P.O. Box 609, Fort Erie, Ontario L2A 5X3

Want to try two free books from another line?
Call 1-800-873-8635 or visit www.ReaderService.com.

* Terms and prices subject to change without notice. Prices do not include applicable taxes. Sales tax applicable in N.Y. Canadian residents will be charged applicable taxes. Offer not valid in Quebec. This offer is limited to one order per household. Not valid for current subscribers to Harlequin® Kimani™ Romance books. All orders subject to credit approval. Credit or debit balances in a customer's account(s) may be offset by any other outstanding balance owed by or to the customer. Please allow 4 to 6 weeks for delivery. Offer available while quantities last.

Your Privacy—The Harlequin® Reader Service is committed to protecting your privacy. Our Privacy Policy is available online at www.ReaderService.com or upon request from the Harlequin Reader Service.

We make a portion of our mailing list available to reputable third parties that offer products we believe may interest you. If you prefer that we not exchange your name with third parties, or if you wish to clarify or modify your communication preferences, please visit us at www.ReaderService.com/consumerchoice or write to us at Harlequin Reader Service Preference Service, P.O. Box 9062, Buffalo, NY 14269. Include your complete name and address.

KROM13R

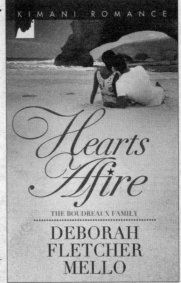